Fly Back and Purify

Mal Foster

"... at last, he said to himself, the spirit has taken up some of the heavy work."

- Leonard Cohen [1934-2016]

© Copyright 2017 by Mal Foster

ISBN: 978-0-244-31608-2

All rights reserved.

This book or any portion thereof may not be reproduced or used in any manner whatsoever without the express written permission of the author or his publisher except for the use of brief quotations in a book review. The right of Mal Foster to be identified as author of this work has been asserted by him in accordance with Section 77 of the Copyright, Designs and Patents Act 1988.

This book is a work of fiction. Names, characters, places and incidents are used fictitiously and are products of the author's imagination. Any resemblance to actual people, living or dead is entirely coincidental.

PublishNation

ABOUT THE AUTHOR

Born in Farnham, Surrey in 1956 Mal Foster is an accomplished poet and local historian. He has also worked as a freelance journalist. In May 2014 he took early retirement to concentrate on his writing and other publishing interests and produced his successful debut historical fiction novel 'The Asylum Soul'. He currently lives in Knaphill near Woking in Surrey and is a great fan of progressive rock music although he turns to the late Canadian singer/songwriter and poet Leonard Cohen when pressed about who and what inspires him.

www.malfoster.co.uk

ACKNOWLEDGEMENTS

Very special thanks to Carol Baker and Richard Cackett.
I would also like to thank those many people who have once again given me their encouragement and suggestions
re: character names etc.
your input has been invaluable and is greatly appreciated.

Cover design by Kit Foster
from a concept by Jason Mulligan

'Things' lyric by Bobby Darin
Copyright © 1962 – Courtesy: Warner/Chappell Music

To Alessandra, as promised…

AUTHOR'S NOTE

I believe there is a valuable therapeutic benefit to be gained from writing and this is something that I have always used as a way of coping with life's often unpredictable challenges. Just prior to the publication of this book I had experienced one of the most beautiful periods of my life, quickly followed by perhaps my darkest ever spell. Seeing the light of day is something we all take for granted so it's quite ironic and unnerving that I have inadvertently chosen the backdrop of mental-health for both of my novels so far. As an author I have at times got into character with those mischievous souls that I've created and I really hope you will enjoy doing the same. Let's see where we go from here…

Thomas (Tommy) Compton, hero. Your name is inscribed in black ink on the first inside page of all these albums, diaries, books. I thumb through numerous photographs of you, a constant grime and grey of fading Kodak imagery. Shy and reserved, unkempt in your younger days. Smart; uniformed, somehow prolific in your latter days with your famous waxed moustache; immaculate coiffure; but with eyes that appear hollow and painfully haunted. Yes, I am talking to you, spiritual family legend and dark star of our ancestral tree.

BOOK ONE

My Aunt Amanda is an eccentric woman. Only in her early sixties but she appears to have fallen old before her time. All this despite an aspiring and promising heyday back in the 1950s, oh yes the 1950s when she modelled French lingerie and donned the front covers of countless fashion magazines. The lipstick she always wore for beauty now replaced by the nicotine stains of countless cigarettes. Capstans, Woodbines or whatever she can get her hands on these days. I love her though; her croaky voice inspires me, reassures me and certainly takes me back to the grey days of what I can only describe as an indifferent childhood but Amanda made it the best she could for me and today I'm visiting her to try and find out more about my father, my grandfather and exactly who I am. The reason for my unusual upbringing has always been a bit of a mystery to me but I believe that getting some positive answers and building my family tree could be just what I need. As usual Amanda tries to avoid talking about my father and changes the subject very quickly when I ask.

'We don't talk about that man in this house,' she always says and today is no different. People hardly mention him but I do know he was called Lionel.

My grandfather was Thomas Compton or Tommy as everyone calls him and was the uncle she adored. She speaks of him with great pride but there's always an element of hesitation in her voice when she starts to utter his name. (Thomas, Tommy, Thomas). She vanishes but then quickly reappears with a large brown suitcase brought down from the attic where she keeps all the artefacts from her colourful past…

'This is Tommy; he's all in here, well sort of.'

I try to grasp exactly what she's trying to say but I guess that she means the suitcase is full of all his paraphernalia. Indeed it's packed full of clothes and lots of books and things.

'This is yours, you can have it now, I think it will fit,' she whispers as she tugs out an old air force flight jacket which was taking up most of the room in the case. It reeks of grubby leather and mothballs.

'During the war, Tommy served with the RAF you know, even learnt to fly a Spitfire, well I think it was a Spitfire but he crashed in the sea off Xlendi. This old jacket was his pride and joy, He loved wearing it, even long after the war was over, loved showing off his squadron's badge,' she said.

I had to ask. 'Where the hell is Xlendi?'

'Malta, well Gozo to be precise, it's one of the Maltese Islands. Tommy was my father Clifford's younger brother, he had a very difficult start to his life and the poor soul was forced into an asylum, the one near Woking for a few years. There was nothing really wrong with him but he was bright and one day he just walked out through the gates and never looked back. He joined the army under a false name and then went into the Royal Air Force when war broke out. His first real job was as a "Chocks Away Man" at Blackbushe Aerodrome in 1942.'

'Chocks Away Man?'

'*Chocks away old boy, got to go and beat Jerry so we can all be home before Christmas!*' she almost sang with a grin.

I was none the wiser at first but then remembered that I had seen the term in one of my old *Commando* comics when I was still a kid. A 'Chocks Away' man was one of the ground-crew.

She then passed me a pile of old letters and some notebooks which were found inside an old biscuit tin. In the tin was a lock of hair, dark red hair, twisted in a sort of plait.

'I've flicked through some of the books, well they're diaries really and there's a long story behind that lock of hair, I've read bits but not all, there is definitely a tragic tale behind it,' she muttered.

I promised her that I would take it all away and read everything when I had time. It's important to know my roots and all about my family history, I owe it to myself to find out as much as I can.

'Look after that stuff, the tin was only brought to me by Mr Meredith a few weeks ago. He's been working at that old asylum I just told you about. It's being demolished. It was found hidden inside a tree they were chopping down. When you read through those things I promise you will find out so much more.'

'Did I ever meet my grandfather?'

'No unfortunately not. He came back to England for your father's funeral in 1966 a few weeks before you were born. He stayed for about a week at your Great Uncle Clifford's house over in Pirbright.'

'Back to England from where?'

'After the war was over he migrated to Malta, lived in a place called Għajnsielem on Gozo. He loved it there and took his wife Katherine who he married a few years after he got out of the asylum. She died of tuberculosis in 1949. It was so sad. When he came back in 1966 he insisted on going to visit the grave of another woman at a churchyard in Tilford on the other side of Farnham not too far from where you live, we went with him. When he found the grave he collapsed to his knees and sobbed for about an hour.'

'Who's grave?'

'That of a young lady, her name escapes me at the moment but she died in 1931. You may find something out in one of his diaries. I think that is actually her lock of hair that was in the tin. Like I said, it is indeed a tragic tale.'

I wonder...

Amanda grabs my arm, 'Look you, I love you like my own son, I am proud of you and of what you have become. Your mother would have been proud as well. If only it had not been for the booze which took her. It's such a shame, such a shame that she left a beautiful lad like you without a mum and never saw you grow up. She would have loved you, you must know that don't you?'

I know some details of my mum's passing but I was only four and most of the other family members have been less than complimentary. They've called her a whore, a pisshead, druggy and things but apparently she never had a great start to life herself. That must be a family thing. A trait as they call it. There's another old story about an Uncle Jack but... I'm Jack. I wonder if that's where my name came from. My mum loved him apparently, even before she met my father but everyone says it was him who caused her to go off the rails. Too many heavy nights of drinking the hard stuff and doing other things like LSD I was told.

I wish I could ask Amanda more about my father. It's all very strange but at the moment I find it prudent not to say anything and considering what's been happening to me just recently, self-preservation is important and the last person I want to upset is Amanda.

She reminded me that it was nearly time for me to go and catch my bus and wished me luck for tomorrow.

Tomorrow is my first day back at work after twelve weeks off sick following my breakdown. The first two weeks were spent in hospital but I feel Okay now, although just a bit apprehensive about going back in the office and facing Nancy Salem, the editor and some of the others. No doubt Geoff Bridger will have his usual say but I don't care, Deborah my counsellor has coached me on how to react. I feel much more confident now but still get the odd negative thought mainly because I over-think and complicate things. 'Self-sabotaging,' I think it's called.

Talking inwardly is something that I do all the time. I rewind my life and then try to move it forward. I diarise things but usually without writing anything down. I try to think things through thoroughly. Analyse, dissect and then hope that I can at least get something right. Complicated? Yes - Effective? No, not really. It's all just simply a narrative to help me think straight.

As usual the bus is late. It's not been the same since the bus company changed and was nationalised. I remember the old buses, the big green ones; I had my first ever kiss on the top deck of one of those on my way home from school when I was five. Amanda collected me from the bus stop that day and I remember her being horrified, not because I kissed a girl, but that I actually kissed a girl with a big crusty yellow sore on her lip.

'You'll catch something nasty if you keep on doing that you silly boy,' I remember her saying.

I must try and sleep properly tonight. Sleep has not been something I can cope with lately, not since the split with Kazkia which caused the breakdown but at least I'm alive to tell the tale. I hate it when self-doubt creeps in and that makes me feel very melancholy.

2

The mirror does not do me any favours. I can feel a sense of paranoia setting in. At nearly twenty-eight, an ageing face with bags under permanently sleepy eyes, the discovery of my first strand of greying hair and then evidence that my whole hairline is slowly receding back. It all depresses me. I wash, I shave and wash again but it doesn't make me feel any better.

I psyche myself up for the day ahead. I mimic positivity whilst almost morphing into a different character, a man in a sharp grey suit. Semi-pretentious and almost armed with what feels like a false demeanour. I bite the bullet as I get ready to go for my train and venture back into the hell-hole that some of us call work.

Walking up the steps towards the office the apprehension creeps back in. My footsteps appear louder as I reach the top. I open the door; it creaks where the catch is stiff. There is a strong smell of coffee which tells me that I'm back. I hang my suit jacket on the hook, walk through the internal door and there is Geoff, feet up, smoking. He looks around.

'Oh look what the cat's dragged in!'

Typically the sort of comment I had expected from him.

'The old girl wants to see you before you sit down,' he said.

By old girl I know he's referring to Nancy, the editor. She's not that old, probably mid-forties but she's the boss and that's a term that Geoff and most of the others use behind her back.

I knock on her office door.

'Come!'

I walk in; she's there with a young girl I haven't seen before.

'This is Lisa Luscombe, our new office junior, she joined us last week. Gillian has left to have her baby and has told me that she won't be coming back.'

'Would you like a coffee?' she asked.

'Yes please.'

'Do you still have it black?'

'Yes, with one sugar!'

'Lisa, would you do the honours please?'

Lisa left the room. There was an uneasy silence as Nancy looked me up and down. I felt as if I was being prepared for the Spanish Inquisition.

'How are you then?' she asked.

'Okay now, I think.'

'Only think? If you're back at work you need to be one-hundred per cent, not half-baked. I need you alert, astute, articulate,' she demanded.

'I am one-hundred per cent.'

'So what's been wrong with you? What's taken you away from me for the past twelve weeks, your sickness certificates didn't tell me anything.'

'I collapsed from depression.' I said rather nervously.

'Depression at your age? You're too young to suffer from depression. So what caused it then?'

This was the bit I've been dreading. Now I have to come clean and be honest about what's really happened.

'I think my marriage break up caused it,' I said.

She paused, took a puff on her cigarette.

'To be honest, you hadn't been right for a long time and something was affecting your work. If you hadn't gone sick I was going to discipline you. We have high standards here. The *Woking Tribune* has a fine reputation and I will not have that compromised by some young upstart who cannot keep his life in check. Do you understand?'

'Yes, I think so,' I replied.

'Again, you're being vague. I want some positive attitude from you otherwise you and I are going to fall out and you'll be looking for a job down at Sainsbury's.'

I felt myself shudder at the thought but then she smiled. Just then Lisa appeared with the coffee.

'Thank you Lisa.'

Lisa smiled and left the room.

'You need to be wary of Geoff when you go back to your desk,' Nancy warned.

'Why?'

'He's not happy that he's been picking up most of your work whilst you've been away. We can't afford to pay the overtime so he's had to put in some honest shifts for a change. He's worked outside his normal hours so don't be surprised if he lays into you a bit.'

I thanked Nancy for the warning. Geoff's probably angry because he's picked up on my normal schedule of mundane stuff like resident's meetings, cake sales and golden wedding anniversaries. All the rubbish we have to report on to try and fill the paper each week.

Nancy said that she would speak to me again on Friday.

'We'll have a drink somewhere after work; just make sure you get your act together and give me something original and presentable to print and please remember to check your punctuation. I am not here to do that for you,' she said as I left her office.

The walk back to the desk was a long one, thankfully Geoff was missing. I noticed it was eleven o'clock already which meant the pub would be open. Geoff's probably in there now in his usual spot at No.1 at the end of the bar. Four pints and then he'll be back. He'll be quite tipsy and almost certainly arrogant. His mouth seems to disappear around to the side of his face when he's been drinking.

I opened my drawer, everything still there including a photograph of Kazkia. I took it from the frame, tore it into quarters and threw it in the bin. It felt like a necessary little ritual that would help me get my life back on track and forget her completely. The 'In Tray' is almost empty. No pending stories, nothing to investigate. Just a note saying that a new computer will be arriving on Wednesday and I still haven't been trained on how to use this one yet!

'Hello, I'm Lisa.'

'Yes I know; I met you in Nancy's office just now.'

'Was your coffee alright?'

'Yes, thank you, great,' I replied.

'You have a meeting tomorrow morning, everyone has to be there,' she said.

'What's it about?'

'Changes in the office.'

'What changes?'

'Ms Salem and Mr Hackett are going to talk about office behaviour and what's got to be done to improve general standards. I've just been typing out the agenda,' she said.

'Who's Mr Hackett?'

'He's the newspaper's new owner, he wants to change everything around, bring the paper out of the dark ages and make it more modern, that's why you're all getting new computers. There's even talk of mobile telephones'.

'What, yuppie phones?'

'Yes those.'

I thought of Geoff. He won't be happy about any of this; he likes to skive while he's out and he'll think that a yuppie phone will act as a tracking device. I doubt if it will stop him from sneaking into a pub all the time though.

'It's not just that,' said Lisa.

'What do you mean?'

She told me that no-one is going to be allowed to drink alcohol during office hours including the lunch break and smoking is going to be banned in the office. Apparently even Nancy isn't happy about that. Morale is going to be so low. I know what Geoff will think. All the others are out working on their stories so the office is very quiet at the moment. Lisa seems quite nice though and she's very good at making coffee. Three cups already now!

'Hello Wazok!' says a familiar voice.

Ted McClymont walks into the office. His dulcet tones unmistakable but at least his greeting is always friendly, in fact his whole personality goes well with his big red face and coiffed white hair. He tells everyone that he used to be a bit of a gang-leader when he was younger.

'We had control back in those days, Stanley Road was our manor and the whole of Maybury was ours, all ours,' he keeps saying.

Now his only 'manor' is his allotment. He often brings in fresh shallots or onions to put in his sandwiches. He cuts them up with a penknife while he's working. Nancy hates it and is always commenting about the smell it creates in the office but he's the senior reporter and he's really good at his job, quite respected actually. Nancy knows it which is probably why she hasn't tried to take it any further.

Ted has just come back from court with a follow up story on the local brothel. 'The Knaphill Knocking Shop' as he calls it. An old woman in her seventies called Lou Marshall has been selling personal services in Sussex Road and the house has since been repossessed by the council.

'She got off with a £200 fine and six months suspended,' he said.

He then pulled me to one side and chuckled.

'There were actually whispers at the back of the court that one of the magistrates was a regular client of hers. He was the one who kept telling us to "Shush", it was all quite funny,' he said.

Ted then asked me if I had met Lisa yet.

'Yes, she makes fantastic coffee,' I replied.

'You sure it's the coffee?'

'What do you mean?'

'Well anyone can put Nescafé and sugar in a cup and add milk and water, it's not rocket science. I'm surprised that a young man like you hasn't attempted to chat her up yet,' he whispered.

'I think she's too nice for that. She's only about seventeen and it's only my first day back and I haven't had a chance to get to know her properly yet.'

'Well if she's old enough to, err... well, you know what I mean.'

Just then Nancy appeared.

'I heard that. That's just the sort of filth that we've got to stamp out in this office. We are a professional business and it's about time all of you started acting in a professional manner. By the way, where's Geoff?'

'Still in the pub probably,' said Ted looking rather ruffled.

I was trying not to laugh. Getting into trouble on my first day back is not a good idea and I think Nancy may have it in for me already. I can't take any chances. She turned around and told us all to be in the meeting room by ten o'clock tomorrow.

'I'll bring some nibbles in,' she said.

'What's this all about?' asked Ted.

'You'll find out tomorrow,' she replied.

Because of my earlier conversation with Lisa I already know. I think tomorrow could be quite an interesting day!

Ted tells us that the problem with covering local news is that sometimes there is often a lack of real news stories. Things can just dry up until someone dies or someone questions another person's weakness and causes a fight. Good news always comes when we are in a position to report the bad news, that's what really sells the paper. We can all sit together in the office and talk about putting the world to rights as much as we like but it won't change anything. All we can really do is keep our eyes and ears open and enhance our role as responsible reporters and hope for that one big story to come along each week. We need to be the architects of our own destiny!'

'Destiny?'

'Yes, destiny!'

Ted was confusing me with his unusual rhetoric.

'Oh the art of creative speaking,' said Nancy as she came back into the office.

3

First coffee of the day and all the talk of the morning is Lisa's short skirt. Ted can't keep his eyes off her and Geoff is being his usual unsavoury self. It's one of those mornings where the banter is quite ripe if not crude. Ted chooses a moment when everyone is eating their sandwiches to mention his prostate problems.

'No-one warns you about how your biological parts can change as you get older,' he said.

'What do you mean?' asked Geoff.

'Well your 'old man' shrinks, your bollocks get bigger and you end up pissing in three different directions all at the same time,' said Ted as he was taking a bite out of his sandwich.

Lisa looked a bit embarrassed and discreetly moved away to the corner by the kitchen.

'So that's why there's always piss on the toilet floor,' quipped Geoff.

To be honest I had wondered that too. Ted just looked up, grinned and then just carried on eating.

Lisa walked back over and reminded us that we had a meeting in five minutes.

Just then the door flung open and Dan and Jasmine walked in. Dan Howarth is the sports reporter who we only see about once a week and Jasmine Patel is the advertising executive. There are a couple of other part-timers but we only see them on Thursdays, our deadline day.

'Has anyone seen the old girl yet?' asked Geoff.

'Yes, she was over the road in the cake shop, I think she's buying us all some treats for the meeting,' Jasmine replied.

'If she's buying us cakes that means there's something up, bad news coming our way,' Geoff said.

Just then a tall gentleman in a beige suit walked in.

'Good morning, I'm Roger Hackett,' he announced.

Nancy suddenly appeared behind him laden with cake boxes.

'Hello all, can you get yourselves off to the meeting room; we'll both be with you in a second,' she shouted.

At the corner of the meeting room was a flip chart, Geoff took a quick look but all the pages were blank.

'Looks like we'll be filling those up, she'll be pinching all our ideas again so she can take the credit. It's going to be another brainstorming session,' he said.

Mr Hackett walked in and formerly introduced himself. He seems friendly enough and sounds quite posh.

'Ms Salem will be taking this meeting, I'm here simply to observe,' he said.

Nancy stood up and looked quite uncomfortable and nervous. I've never seen her like that before.

'Right, can anyone in here tell me what being politically correct means?' she asked.

We all looked around at each other but there was just silence.

'Come on, one of you must be able to tell me.'

Geoff put his hand up and said, 'Is it voting Labour?'

Everyone laughed. Nancy looked annoyed and embarrassed.

Just then Mr Hackett interrupted.

'I can see we have some problems here with attitude. There's probably a bit of naiveté too. Let me explain. This newspaper needs to behold higher standards. We are putting out a great product but it could be better. Some of our articles are a bit too opinionated. They need to be more transparent, rational and concise. Some recent items appear vague and even important information such as locations and dates are missing. It's sloppy. The best way we can move forward is by improving our general standards here in the office. Nancy, please take back over!'

'Yes, we are going to adopt a new office 'Political Correctness Policy' as standard. It will act as a basic rule book for all our office procedures and behavioural standards. The policy has been written and young Lisa will be typing it up for me this week. You will each be given a copy which must be signed for.'

'What's in it?' asked Ted.

'Well that's why we're here now. I will explain all the main points and Mr Hackett and I will be pleased to answer any questions.

'I will have loads of those, don't you worry,' said Geoff.

'Okay, the first issue we need to tackle is the language and banter that goes on in the office. It's bad, it's rude, it's uncouth, and most of all, it's totally unnecessary. It gets worse in the afternoon, usually after you all get back from the pub, so, from next Monday, no-one will be allowed to drink alcohol during work time and that includes your lunch breaks.

'But we don't get paid for our lunch breaks so how can you tell us what we can and can't do during that time?' said Geoff.

'We have evidence that alcohol has been affecting the quality of work and general behaviour for some time,' said Nancy.

'Where's that evidence come from then, who's been snitching?'

'No-one's been snitching as you put it. Observations have been made over a period of three months and it's clear that many things need to improve. Another thing we need to stamp out is racist remarks. I do not want to hear words like nigger, paki or chinky in the office anymore. If I hear anyone using those words they will be disciplined and instant dismissal is more than likely.'

'But I was brought up to call a Spade a Spade and a Coon a Coon,' said Geoff who was now beginning to get quite angry.

Everyone else was lowering themselves down into their seats, me included.

'Is it true that smoking is going to be banned in the office as well?' Ted asked.

'Yes, again from next Monday. The handyman will be coming in at the weekend to transform the old store room into a smoking room. There will be a table and four chairs and a couple of ashtrays. That's the only place you will be allowed to smoke.'

'So it's not a total ban,' said Geoff.

'No, you just won't be allowed to smoke in the office at your desks or anywhere else apart from the designated smoking area anymore,' she said.

Mr Hackett stood up.

'One more thing, I would like to see all you men wearing a tie next time I'm here, if I have to, I will bring a box of my old ones in so there can be no excuses.'

I could see Geoff beginning to get very agitated.

'Excuse me Sir, but we are journalists not bank clerks,' he said.

Mr Hackett glared in Geoff's direction.

'Well, if you don't like it there's a Labour Exchange just down the road.' Geoff sunk down into his chair without answering.

After the meeting everyone tucked into Nancy's cakes whilst Lisa brought in the teas and coffees. Geoff had disappeared almost certainly to the pub which is just around the corner. I definitely think The Albion would go bust if it wasn't for him and it probably will after next week when he has to stop drinking during his lunch break.

Lisa came over to me and asked how I was which was a bit strange. It's not because she fancies me or anything or at least I don't think so. I think someone has said something to her about why I was off sick. She appears to be quite curious but I do wonder why she wants to find out more about me, perhaps Ted is trying to play Cupid? I saw him chatting with her earlier.

4

The office is empty. Nancy's away on a seminar, Geoff's out covering a car accident and Ted is back at court watching over a fraud case. Jasmine may be in later and that's it. It's Wednesday, I've been back three days and not even a sniff of a story has landed on my desk. Perhaps I need to go out and find one, invent a story perhaps but that would fall short of etiquette and professionalism and would probably get me the sack.

As I anticipated Lisa has been round about me all morning. Endless cups of coffee and a number of inquisitive looks. She's very intelligent though and she comes across as very caring but I'm not sure what her motive is. Maybe I should ask.

A little later she comes over again.

'Are you Okay? You look a bit down,' she said.

'I'm feeling fine thank you, I'm just a bit frustrated that no real stories are coming my way. It doesn't look good. I want to be active and it doesn't feel very productive. I can imagine what my next appraisal will be like if this carries on,' I replied.

'Don't worry, everything will work out for you soon,' she said with a smile.

'So, what do you do in your spare time?' I thought I'd ask.

'Oh I dance.'

'What kind of dance?'

'Ballet, I love to dance ballet,'

'Where?'

'I belong to a group in Brookwood; I go with my best friend Trudy. She's from up north and works in a solicitor's office here in Woking. She actually prefers belly dancing but you won't catch me doing that! We practice every Saturday morning in the church hall, we put on two shows in the spring and autumn and visit the garden fêtes at the old people's homes in the summer. I love dancing,' she said.

'Have you been doing it very long?'

'Since I was about ten, my mother used to dance. She took me to London to see a show one day and I was hooked. I absolutely love dancing, all forms of dancing,' she said.
'Except belly dancing obviously,' I joked.
'Now you're being silly.'
'Yes, perhaps I am,' I laughed.
'Do you always laugh at your own jokes?'
'It wasn't a joke!'
Now she was making me feel stupid and I began to wonder why she really came over to speak. I know it's quiet in the office today but I've only known her since Monday, it feels like she knows more about me than she's been letting on. I wonder who's been talking. I decided to ask again.

'No, no-one, it's just in my nature to ask lots and lots of questions, I'm a bit nosey like that. I like to get to know what makes people tick, what makes up their personal fabric,' she said.

I hadn't heard that expression before and I told her that she had a very mature outlook for someone her age.

'Oh no don't get me wrong, I love going out to discos and I love music, I love going to concerts and festivals and things.'

'What sort of music do you like?'

'I love all sorts, rock music mainly but I don't like to pigeon-hole what I hear. If I like it, I like it and that's fine with me,' she said.

Just as I was about to reply the door opened and Geoff staggered in. He'd been in the pub on the way back from the accident.

'That wasn't very nice, I needed a stiff drink after seeing that,' he said.

'Why was somebody killed?' Lisa asked.

'No, I just didn't like seeing a nice 1977 S plate Alfa Romeo written off,' he replied.

Lisa and I just both looked at each other and rolled our eyes. Typical Geoff I thought. I wonder what he's going to do next week when he can't drink anymore.

5

'Another day, another dollar.'

Every day someone in the office has to say it and this time it was Dan's turn. He only pops in every so often so I suppose that he thinks that he's being original. He's never about any other time to hear anyone else say it.

Geoff's been in but he had an 'episode' on the way to work and has gone down the market to buy a new pair of under pants.

'Too much Guinness again last night probably,' Ted said.

I laugh!

The office is busier with it being deadline day but the new computers have caused a problem because the disks are incompatible. We've all had to plug the old ones back in so that we can get the copy over to Beryl. She needs to process the final templates and get them ready for the courier to take them to the printers in Aldershot. It's the only job she does which is why we only normally see her on Thursdays. There's a big risk as well because she's the only one who knows what to do.

'Nancy knows,' said Ted.

'Oh well, that's a relief!' shrieked Beryl.

She's a bit hard of hearing but always seems to notice when someone's talking about her.

'Selective hearing I think,' whispered Ted.

At last I have a story to cover. They've just opened a new supermarket in Knaphill and I need to be there for eleven o'clock. I'm meeting Tony the photographer there. He's another one who hardly comes into the office; he's got his own dark room at his house in Oriental Road and usually drops his photographs off here after we've all gone home.

Nancy came into the office just now and looked very anxious. She's knows everything is running late because of the computer situation. If we miss the deadline she'll have to inform Mr Hackett which is obviously something she wants to avoid.

'If the deadline is missed we will miss our slot at the printers, the papers will come out late and sales are affected,' she took no hesitation in reminding us.

Now I've got to catch the train to Brookwood and walk up to Knaphill. At least I'll be getting some fresh air today. It feels great at last to have my journalist's head back on.

6

Today has been the best day of the week for me. I submitted my supermarket story from yesterday. Nancy seemed happy with it even though I used commas instead of semi-colons in a couple of places.

'You're getting there,' she said.

I'll take that, it could have been worse and to be honest I was expecting her to be more critical.

She reminded me that she was taking me for a drink this evening. I was hoping that she had forgotten. It's been a very long and exhausting week and I should just go home and lie down on my bed and relax. I have a weekend appointment back at the hospital clinic with Deborah my counsellor at ten o'clock tomorrow and I need to be ready for that. She will have the results from the last round of tests they did on me so I am a bit worried about it all.

We leave the office at five o'clock on Fridays, Poet's Day as everyone calls it.

Nancy took me around to her car at the back of the office. It's a bright green Citroën 2CV which she tells me she is very proud of.

'I've had it since 1982,' she said.

It reminds me of an upturned pram but I decided not to tell her what I was thinking. After all, self-preservation must always come first with me these days. In the car the floor is covered in cigarette ends. It doesn't look like she's emptied the ashtray for weeks. In fact, the whole inside of the car looks and smells like an ashtray.

'Excuse the mess, just hold on tight and enjoy the ride,' she said.

'So where are we going?'

'There's a little pub near where I live called the Hare and Hounds, I'll take you there and then drive you to the train station afterwards,' she said.

'I could take you all the way home if you like,' she added.

I declined her offer, I just want to have that drink and be on my way as soon as possible and I don't really want her visiting my pokey little bedsit in Farnham.

At the pub there was a barman called Martin who I recognised but didn't know very well. I think he used to drink in another pub over my way a few years ago.

He kept winking and then said, 'It must be your turn tonight!'

I got the gist of what he was saying and I wasn't sure if Nancy had heard him.

We found a corner at the back of the pub by the French doors. I had a pint of cider and Nancy had a large glass of white wine, *Pinot Grigio* I think it's called.

She started asking what had happened between me and Kazkia; I didn't really want to talk about it all but she kept pressing. I know she didn't like her very much but they had only met once before I joined the paper so I didn't think that Nancy should be entitled to her opinion.

'Come on, you can tell me, we're not in work now and we are both adults aren't we?' she kept saying.

I had to keep changing the subject to avoid talking about my marriage failure and eventually found myself on the fourth pint of cider. The adrenalin was still pumping but I felt less nervous. The cider must have helped me to relax.

'What will be, will be,' I thought.

I noticed that Nancy had started slurring all her words and Martin the barman and one of the barmaids were laughing as they looked over from the bar hatch, just then a bell rung.

'Last orders at the bar,' someone shouted.

I looked at my watch, I hadn't realised the time, I hadn't even noticed that it was dark outside and that it was nearly eleven o'clock. Kicking out time!

Martin came over and pointed at Nancy.

'Can you walk her home mate? She's too pissed to drive, her car will be alright here; she quite often leaves it in our car park on a Friday night.'

Now I was feeling a bit trapped. No lift to the station, the last bus had already gone and it was too far to walk all the way home and I didn't have enough money for a taxi.

'So you're taking me home young man, I'll show you where the coffee is.' Nancy said.

Martin interrupted. 'That's her house down the road on the corner, have fun,' he said and laughed.

By now everyone was looking. I got the impression that Nancy had often done this sort of thing before.

When we reached her doorstep she had trouble finding her key and was fumbling for a cigarette.

'Sorry I couldn't give you a lift, I'm a bit drunk.'

We went into the hallway; there was a small black dog which needed feeding. She made a fuss of it before sitting down on the stairs and giving it a big hug.

'Meet Stella,' she said.

She then led me to the kitchen, fed the dog some dry food and poured us both a glass a water.

'Drinking water when I get home always helps me sober up more quickly,' she added.

By now her voice was starting to sound more coherent again but I was still worried about what was going to happen next.

'Right,' she said while banging her hand down on the kitchen table.

'It looks like I'm stuck with you for the rest of the night, now you can show me what kind of man you are,' she said with half a smile.

She grabbed me, pulled my tie off and then tugged my collar.

'Come on, I'll show you my lovely new bed.'

We went upstairs and into her bedroom. Her bed had a leather headboard, with a built-in radio and a tea maker to one side.

'This was my treat to myself when my husband walked out' she said.

'Husband?'

'Yes husband, don't worry, he hasn't been on the scene for quite awhile now.'

I wasn't sure how to react. I wasn't finding Nancy very attractive at all. Her greasy blond hair which is dyed with random blue and purple streaks and her shocking pink dress clashed with her green stockings. Her dress sense is always rather odd. What a mess, I was thinking. Just then she pushed her hand inside my shirt.

'Take it off,' she demanded.

I hesitated.

'Take it off,' she said again.

I decided to comply and couldn't help thinking about the consequences on Monday morning if I didn't go along with what was happening.

She pushed me on to her bed and then rolled me on top of her.

'Undress me you little bastard,' she demanded.

I pulled the dress off over her head. Her bra had a catch on the front and while I was undoing that she took her stockings off and pulled her knickers down. She rolled me over again and pulled my pants and trousers off.

Her body was quite unlovely. Not fat but there was lots of loose skin hanging down from where she'd lost weight, lots of creases and spots and warts and other marks. I wanted to back out but it was too late. I was definitely at a point of no return.

'Come on then you little worm, fuck me,' she screamed out enthusiastically in some kind of anticipation.

I just wanted to run away but I knew that somehow I would have to perform.

Eventually I got there, a couple of thrusts and a shudder and then I heard her groaning. This really wasn't sex at its best. It was a chore and I felt disgusted with myself, quite sick actually. Even sex with Kazkia was sometimes better than this!

'Pass me my cigarettes,' she demanded.

'Seven minutes! About average for a young man your age,' she said as she lit up.

I smiled at her albeit falsely, pretending that I had enjoyed the experience. I really hoped that she wasn't going to expect it all over again.

First bus out of here in the morning, like something in a book I'd once read I thought…

Time to get up and go home
to the call of the wild and dawn chorus
Time to get up and go home
before she awakes and asks who I am
Time to get up and go home

*and examine the need for a conscience
Time to get up and go home
escape on the first bus of the morning
Time to get up and go home
and murder a steaming black coffee
Time to get up and go home
before the day becomes even more merciless
Time to get up and go home
and figure out what all of this is.*

7

The meeting with Deborah my counsellor today has been worrying me all week. I feel tired now after only just surviving last night. I feel that I need to recover my senses, brush myself down and start all over again.

'How have you been, Jack?' She looked quite concerned.

It was the kind of look you receive when there's bound to be some bad news coming.

'We had a good look at you while you were here, didn't we?' she said.

'Yes, you probably did,' I replied rather nervously.

'Well it's not all bad news. How's your first week back at work been?'

'Better than expected.'

'How did you feel on the first day?'

'Apprehensive.'

'Was it daunting?'

'Yes almost definitely.'

'How did your boss treat you?'

'She was stern but fair and warned me that I could have lost my job and still could if things don't improve.'

'Is she aware of your condition?'

'I'm not even aware of a condition apart from the fact that I had the bloody breakdown.'

'Sorry, silly question.'

I was beginning to feel uncomfortable with all the questions but I thought that there must be a reason why she was asking. She said that I was looking very tired but I felt it best not to mention what had happened last night. I didn't really want to talk about it, especially not to her!

'Is there any record of mental illness in your family?' Deborah asked.

'What do you mean?'

'Have any of your family members been diagnosed with psychological issues before?'

I was about to say 'No' but then I remembered that my grandfather had been forced to live in an asylum when he was younger so I decided to tell her.

'Well my grandfather was in an asylum when he was in his twenties, I've only very recently found that out,' I said.

'Diagnosed with what?'

'I don't know. All I know is that he was sent to the Brookwood Asylum when he was around twenty-three years old. That would have been about 1929,' I said.

'Can you try and find out what was wrong with him? We may be able to tell from that if your condition is indeed a hereditary one,' she asked.

'I'll try; my Aunt Amanda gave me a lot of his books and things from around about that time when I visited her recently but she did say that there was nothing wrong with him, he was there by mistake.'

'Well it's important that you find out what you can,' she said.

'So please, please, can you tell me what's actually wrong with me though?'

'Given all the tests and results from your screenings we've concluded that you suffer from an acute form of depression brought on by anxiety and paranoia. There's also evidence to suggest that you may be a borderline schizophrenic.'

'Can you please remind me what that is?'

'It's a split personality disorder which may explain why you often talk to yourself, do you still do that?

'Err yes, only in my own head but not out loud.'

'Are you sure?'

'Yes I'm completely sure.'

'You will need to go away and find out as much information as you can about your grandfather. Health conditions can often skip a generation or two. If he's suffered from certain things when he was younger you could have the same problems. If we can find out what those were then we may be able to help you that little bit more.'

Deborah doesn't normally work on Saturdays and she'd given up her own time just to speak with me. Much of what she was saying was beginning to make sense and that was beginning to worry me. I think I will spend tomorrow going through Tommy's things. Perhaps I may find some answers.

I've decided that this would be my last visit to see Deborah and talk about what she calls mental illness. I refuse to be labelled that way. I know I am not mental, yes, different, alternative maybe but I am definitely not mental!

8

Going through Tommy's things the diaries are certainly the most interesting. His writing is hard to read, some of it is almost in hieroglyphics. Lots of pages are missing as if the books have been censored. I phoned Amanda and she told me that they were like that when Mr Meredith gave them to her.

'Mr Meredith was handed that old tin by one of his workers who had found it covered in rust but well preserved inside a tree hollow. When he looked at the contents he recognised our family name and the address on some of the letters so brought it over to me the same evening,' she said.

I asked her where the tree was.

'In the grounds of the old lunatic asylum where your grandfather used to be, remember I told you that they're knocking it all down to build a new supermarket and houses.'

The supermarket is already open, that's the story I covered on Thursday and Amanda seemed surprised when I told her.

I asked her about the missing pages. She wasn't aware but she did say that Mr Meredith had read everything and may have removed them so that she wouldn't get upset.

'He did say that some bits were quite harrowing but I couldn't find them,' she said.

Mr Meredith is an old family friend who has his own tree surgery and landscaping firm. Perhaps I need to get hold of him to try and find out why he's ripped some of the pages out.

Looking through what's left of the diaries it does seem that some bad things were happening but it's hard to tell. I can't even find out what was wrong with Tommy although I can see that he had a speech defect and he talks of being accused of suffering from delusions and being melancholy. Melancholy means sad or depressed. A word Deborah kept using when I first came out of hospital. He also talks of a girl called Maisie and I've found a Katherine. That must be the one Amanda told me about who he married and who's buried somewhere in Malta.

The flight jacket fits but an oddity is that Amanda told me that he flew Spitfires in the war but the badge on the jacket belongs to RAF 29 Squadron. That's a Mosquito bomber squadron. In the jacket pocket I found an official RAF Accident Card. It looks like Tommy was actually a navigator and may have survived being shot down by the Luftwaffe…

'RAF Operations (Malta) heard from HK147 when it was at 10,000 feet after completing a 'Ground Control Interception' (GCI) practice and indications were that the aircraft was attacked by rogue bandits under cover of bright sunlight, assumed aircraft caught fire and out of control, pulled out too violently, aircraft breaking up at once. One crew member killed and the other bailed out safely.'

I also found a photograph of Tommy wearing the flight jacket; it is indeed the same one so I don't know where Amanda got her story of the Spitfire from. Maybe she just got her planes mixed up. The back of the photograph is dated Malta, 17th April, 1943. After spending nearly the whole day indoors going through his things, I've been intrigued by the life of my grandfather. I can almost smell him, breathe him. I feel like he may be watching over me but I guess that's wishful thinking.

I'm sitting by the open window, listening to one of my favourite Pink Floyd albums. The music helps me to relax. My mind drifts and takes me back to an age when Tommy was still alive, incarcerated at the asylum perhaps and then in contrast I think about the conflict of the Second World War, the Mediterranean, I can only imagine what it must have been like for him. I really want to get to know him better. I want to know more about his war time activities and what happened to him afterwards. I must remember that I also need to find out all I can about my father because he's the man who connects us both!

9

Monday morning and the strong intrusive smell of nail polish remover.

'I need to make my nails pink again,' Lisa said with a smile.

Geoff just groaned while Ted asked when the next cup of coffee was landing on his desk.

'In a minute, in a minute I just need to let my nails dry first.'

'Hang on; if you're taking the polish off, why do you need to wait for your nails to dry?' asked Geoff.

'It's because I've already started putting my new polish on; silly.'

'Don't you dare call me "silly" you dozy little tart,' Geoff snapped.

That was enough to put Lisa in tears and she rushed off to the toilet.

'You've done it now, we'll all be making our own coffee this morning at this rate,' laughed Ted.

Nancy came out of her office to ask what all the noise was about. It was the first time I've seen her since I left her house early on the Saturday morning and I tried to keep my head down. I think she noticed.

'Good morning Jack, did you have a nice weekend?' she asked.

'Err, yes thank you.'

'Get up to much?'

'This and that.'

'Don't tell me, Friday night was the big highlight.'

Geoff perked up, 'didn't you both out for a drink?'

'Yes, we did and it was a very pleasant evening too, wasn't it Jack,' she said.

'Err yes, it was,' I replied rather sheepishly.

'Where's Lisa?'

'Oh, Geoff just upset her, called her a tart and she ran off to the loo,' said Ted.

'Let me remind you all that this is the first day of our new office standards policy and I will not tolerate any bad behaviour. You're all grown men and you should be treating that young lady with respect.

She's new and she's keen and I can't afford to lose her simply because one of you lot can't behave. Oh, and Geoff remember that there's no pub for you anymore, not until after work anyway.'

Geoff growled.

Nancy then went off to the toilet to check on Lisa while Ted got up to make the coffee.

'Right, how do you do this again?' he joked.

There hasn't been much going on in Woking over the last few days so everyone is hungry for stories. Sometimes it gets to the point where we're phoning around for news or 'padding out' as Geoff calls it. To be fair he's pretty good at turning a mundane craft show into an epic feature length headliner though.

Nancy came back into the office with Lisa.

'She's Okay now but no thanks to you lot, now look after her,' she said.

'Great timing, now that I've just made all the coffees,' quipped Ted.

Nancy just glared at him.

I was wondering if Nancy was going to say any more to me about Friday night, I hoped not.

After things had died down and calm was restored Lisa came over for a chat.

'Sorry I got a bit upset this morning,' she said.

'It wasn't your fault no-one's got the right to call you that.'

'It doesn't matter, I shouldn't have called him "Silly", so I probably deserved to be called a dozy tart,' she said.

I just smiled.

'What happened between you and Nancy after work on Friday, did you go for a drink?'

'Err yes,' I replied.

'Did anything else happen?'

'Err no.'

'I bet it did. I know it did because you're starting to blush.'

'No it didn't.'

'Liar, liar, pants on fire,' Lisa sang.

'Was it good?'

'No it bloody well wasn't,' I snapped.

'Got yah, got yah,' Lisa shouted.

Fortunately by now everyone else was out of the office.

'Don't worry, it's our little secret, I won't tell anyone,' she promised.

Now I felt very embarrassed. I was also a bit angry that I had allowed myself to be caught out. I wonder what Lisa must think of me now?

10

This morning I have witnessed the start to a different kind of day. Ted came back from the magistrate's court in a kind of frenzy and wanted to find out what the word 'recalcitrant' meant. One of the magistrates had used it in the summing up at the case he's been covering.

'First time I've ever heard that word and not even sure how to spell it,' he said.

Geoff, Lisa and I all stopped what we were doing and went over to the shelf where the dictionaries are kept. We have at least ten dictionaries in the office.

'One of us should be able to find it,' said Geoff.

It was rare to see him actually behaving like a team member for once; maybe his enforced lack of alcohol intake was slowly turning him into a human-being I thought.

After a couple of hours we were all still looking.

'Has anyone found out how to spell it?' asked Lisa.

'Well if we knew that we wouldn't be looking would we,' snapped Geoff.

'Actually, it's not just the spelling, I need to find out what the word means,' said Ted as he tried to diffuse another confrontation.

'Fair point but I think I've found it now,' said Geoff looking all pleased with himself.

'Recalcitrant, blimey that word has five syllables; our readers won't be able to cope with that.'

'So what does the word actually mean?' asked Ted.

'It means having an obstinately non co-operative attitude towards authority or discipline,' said Geoff.

'Oh the irony, oh and by the way, it's only four syllables,' shouted Lisa gleefully.

'Steady on,' I thought. This is another one of those conversations that could quite easily get out of hand.

Lisa then asked Ted what case he had been covering at court.

'The school case, where a child was supposedly unfairly punished for not adhering to classroom instructions and his parents verbally abused and threatened his teacher the following day. The father got a heavy fine for breach of the peace and threatening behaviour, the mother got off while the little bugger's been placed at a another school,' he said.

'Anyone for coffee now?' asked Lisa.

I realised that we had all wasted nearly three hours trying to find out what one word meant. We're all supposed to be professional journalists so it did kind of make me laugh.

This afternoon I'm going down to the Military Cemetery at Brookwood. The Americans are there doing some sort of commemoration.

At the cemetery there is a quiet stillness about the place even though I can hear the sound of distant voices coming from behind the trees as I walk over from the station. It's an eerie place, even in the daytime under bright sunlight. Rabbits clatter among the gravestones and spook me a little, shadows fall short from the tall trees, red cedars I think, the smell of incense burning from somewhere. I struggle to compose myself. Tony has lent me his camera for the afternoon. I'm the photographer as well as a reporter today. No double wages though I thought! When I arrive at the American section there are three soldiers in US Marine uniform, a policeman and a few men in suits and some women all dolled-up. An old woman scurries out of the office.

'Are you from the *Tribune*?'

'Yes I am, I'm Jack Compton.'

'Compton, oh, that's a nice local name.'

'Would you like a glass of lemon squash?'

'Err, yes please.'

'I'll tell the organisers that you're here.'

She went off and then came back with a short balding man dressed in a maroon suit and white spats. He looked very flustered and spoke very fast.

'So what is the commemoration all about today?' I asked.

He hesitated, reached inside his suit jacket pocket and pulled out some notes.

'Oh yes, it's the anniversary of the first American soldier being buried at the cemetery today. The Americans like to use the word interred,' he said.

'Is there a photographer?'

'I'm taking the pictures today, our usual photographer is away covering another story,' I replied.

'Well let's hope you're good at taking photographs,' he mumbled as he led me over to where the proceedings were about to start.

'Obnoxious little git,' I thought.

Back home I reflect on the day. Happy now that I've got a couple of stories under my belt since being back at work.

11

In the office, Lisa is crying.
'Why are you crying?'
'I don't know.'
She tells me that she has a broken heart.
'Why is it broken?'
'I don't know.'
'Boyfriend?'
'Yes, boyfriend.'
'Did he love you?'
'I don't know.'
'Did you love him?'
'I don't know.'

I guessed that Lisa needed to be left alone but then her mood changed and she glanced at me with a smile…

'Time for me to find out some more things about you now,' she said.

'So where's Kazkia from?'

The question came completely out of the blue and I was certainly not expecting it.

'What do you mean, where's she's from?'
'What country?
'She's English.'
'I thought Kazkia was foreign.'
'No she's definitely English.'
'Kazkia is not an English name though is it.'
'No it's not, it's a made up name.'
'Made up?'
'Yes, made up.'
'I don't understand.'

'Kazkia's real name is Karen. She just didn't like her birth name so one day some years ago she just changed it and sort of reinvented herself. She's still called Karen on all her official documents like on her birth certificate and on her driving licence.'

'Well that's silly, what made her do that?'

'She likes to be different and she's also a bit of a snob, she felt that Karen was too much like a housing estate name, a bit common like Sharon or Tracey. Apparently she wanted something that sounded a bit more exotic.'

'What was she like? Describe her.'

'Thin, very thin in fact.'

'What, anorexic?'

'No not that thin, just a bit on the scrawny side.'

'What colour eyes and hair?'

'Deep blue eyes, I always liked blue eyes and that was what really attracted me to her in the first place, as for her hair, well her hair colour and length changed all the time and still does I think. Each week she used to have it styled and dyed differently. She was a bit like a chameleon really.'

'So what went wrong between you two?'

'To be honest it was probably never right from the start, perhaps I should never have got involved with her in the first place and I've been regretting it ever since. She already had a reputation for sleeping around. I thought I could change her. Just after we got married I was tipped off by one of her friends that she was seeing someone she had met through a lonely hearts column. She started disappearing off in her little white car to Guildford and other places and not coming back until about three in the morning. She always said that she had been with friends but as it turned out, many of those so-called friends didn't even exist. It was then that I realised there was a problem. It became obvious that she was back up to her old tricks when someone she was supposed to be out with one evening phoned and asked to speak to her. That's when I knew the relationship was effectively over.'

'Who was she carrying on with then?'

'Some guy from Godalming; there were probably others too. I shouldn't really care. The whole thing eventually drove me to despair. I ended up with twelve weeks off work suffering from an acute form of depression. I can't believe I let that woman control my life so much, I can kick myself really. Anyway I don't want to talk about it anymore, I've told you enough already.'

Lisa apologised.

'Sorry, it's just in my nature to keep asking questions, I like to know all about people and their relationships and how they work, it helps me,' she said.

Lisa always seems very inquisitive. Today she's been asking too many questions though. I've felt uncomfortable talking about it. I'm trying to move on but Lisa keeps saying that talking about things will help. I'm not so sure.

The work today had been slow. In fact there was no work! Nancy had gone out to dinner with a 'gentleman friend' and didn't come back. Ted went to Guildford to cover a new story at the court and I think Geoff just sneaked off to the pub.

After work I rushed home as fast as I could; I felt an impulse to go through more of Tommy's things. I kept going back to his diaries, three of them from his days in the asylum. I was trying to piece together what life was like for him in there. I got the distinct impression that he should never have been sent there in the first place. I can see that he liked working on the pig farm and talks about a Knaphill Pie made from the bacon. There is a recipe for the pie tucked in the back of one of the diaries. I also found his marriage certificate. He married Katherine in Aldershot in 1938. With the certificate was her discharge letter from the Brookwood Lunatic Asylum dated 14th February 1932. I also found a strange letter Tommy had written to himself. When he joined the army under a false name it looks like he called himself Thomas O'Leary but changed it back to Compton when he joined the RAF.

Apart from the RAF Accident Card I couldn't find out too much more about his time in the air force although there is a small green travel document which gave him free passage to Malta just after the war. There are a few other photographs of him in his uniform standing in front of a wooden hut with some other airmen; they're all smoking pipes and look quite happy.

12

I'm still waiting for my first big story. Geoff and Ted always seem to get all the cream. I've never covered a court story before and Nancy has asked Ted to take me along to show me the ropes and the protocol. Protocol is not a word that is commonly used so I found that quite amusing.

'Well it's not as if we're covering the Royals is it,' quipped Geoff.

Nancy told us that we have a new reporter joining us on Monday and has reminded us to all to be respectful.

'She's from the middle-east, no actually half of her is, her father is Iranian and her mother is English. She's a Muslim girl and wears a scarf,' Nancy told us.

'What's her name?' Lisa asked.

'Clarissa.'

'That's a nice name.'

'Why do we need another reporter? There's not enough work for us as there is,' said Geoff.

'Actually Mr Hackett wants to build for the future, he wants to make the *Tribune* a diverse newspaper and by employing someone from an ethnic minority he hopes to achieve that,' Nancy informed us.

'Bloody foreigners coming over here and pinching all our jobs,' said Geoff rather angrily.

'Well if she's half English then she's not really a foreigner is she?' said Lisa.

I sensed that this was potentially going to be another one of those fiery conversations.

'Just be nice to her and treat her with respect, I'm sure she'll fit in well. Oh and by the way Geoff if I have to sack anybody, then I will already have a ready-made replacement!'

Geoff didn't respond to what Nancy had just said but I could tell he wasn't happy. He just wandered back to his desk and lit a cigarette.

'Put it out!' screamed Nancy.

'You know you can't do that in the office anymore.'

Geoff got up, glared at Nancy and then went outside.

Ted had just got back from covering a demonstration by residents in Horsell who were opposed to a new development of houses and flats.

'That was the worst morning I've ever had in my whole journalistic career. I couldn't wait to get away from there. I hate having to deal with people like that. Green *Barbour* welly-wearing do-gooders with up their own arse attitudes and la-di-da voices. They were just full of their own self-importance, fucking snobs,' he said.

I'd never heard Ted swear before but his little rant did seem to take the tension away from the conversation we just had with Nancy about the new girl coming next week.

At home despite being the middle of summer the room is quite cold. I sit and think about the day and then wonder about Tommy again. It feels like he's looking over me and that I'm getting to know him but I must make sure that he's not just another made up voice in my head. It's almost like having a ghost for a friend although I haven't seen him yet and I keep thinking about what Deborah said. She called me a borderline schizophrenic!

13

There were two empty wine bottles down by the bed on the floor this morning and my head feels sore… I remember it was Nancy who said something about drinking tap water to help sober up. Water, black coffee and then more water might do the trick I thought.

The office is empty again today, Geoff is out covering a new farmers' market co-operative down in Chobham and Ted is back at court this time on a celebrity shoplifting case. Lisa thankfully is busy working on the new office policy document revision so hasn't had too much time for idle chit-chat. To be honest I can do without more of her searching questions about my private life. I do like her though but only as a work colleague, nothing more than that. She's far too young for me and my life has been complicated enough, particularly over the last few months.

Jasmine came into the office and asked me if I had met the new girl Clarissa yet.

'No I think she's gone somewhere for her induction today,' I said.

She's my best friend's daughter, she's a lovely girl but I'm worried about how Geoff might treat her, I know he's got a hidden agenda when it comes to ethnic minorities and things,' she said.

I couldn't help but agree with her. She then started asking questions about what had happened between me and Kazkia.

'If you don't mind, Lisa has already given me the third degree and I don't really want to go through it all again and by the way it's private,' I said.

Jasmine looked at me a bit funny.

'So Lisa who has only been here for five minutes gets the full run down and I get nothing. I thought I was your friend,' she said.

Lisa looked over and glared but then just carried on with her typing.

'You are my friend!' I told Jasmine.

'Don't worry; I'm only messing with you,' she said.

'As if I really need people messing with my head,' I thought.

Jasmine eventually shut up and got on with her work. It was just then that Nancy appeared.

'Hey Jack how about a drink after work tomorrow evening?' she asked.

'Err, no thanks, I've already got plans for tomorrow and the weekend,' I replied quite hastily.

Of course I was being a bit economical with the truth which is something I never feel comfortable with but again it was a self-preservation thing.

'Don't worry, I thought you might have, I'm only kidding,' she said.

'Blimey,' I thought, they're all at it today, if things carry on like this I'll be back in the nuthouse by Monday and none of it would have been my fault.

At lunchtime I walked across the road to the sandwich shop. It's called *The Sandwich Emporium* for some reason, a name I have never really understood. A sandwich is a sandwich and as long it contains cheese and onion I'm usually happy. In the queue just behind me was Deborah. I felt awkward as we stopped for a quick chat outside.

'Are you still coming to see me next Saturday,' she asked.

'I was going to phone you and cancel.'

'Why?'

'Well since our last meeting I've been trying to sort things out in my head, a lot of that has been done by using some of your helpful advice. I now feel happy analysing and challenging things and I feel more positive. I also have a new interest. I'm researching my family tree and it's been very interesting to find out things about the life of my grandfather and that's been helping me quite a lot.'

'But the big question is, are you still talking to yourself and beating yourself up inside. Are you still experiencing those long moments of anxiety and depression?'

'I'm still talking to myself a bit, analysing things but not out loud. I'm definitely not beating myself up anymore and to be honest I think I'm just generally coping with life Okay now.'

'That's good, really good, here's my number again if you need it, I'm only a phone call away, if you need to just call,' she said.

I thanked her for the chat and we shook hands. She gave me a hug and a little kiss on the cheek. I feel now that if I'm going to move on

I need to detach myself from people like Deborah even though I know she's been doing her best to help me. She's a good caring person so I do appreciate everything she's done but sometimes all this talk about being mental and stuff makes me feel worse.

14

We were all wondering where Geoff was this morning as Nancy came out into the office with the new girl Clarissa.

'Two things, please welcome Clarissa Batmanghelidjh to the fold, she knows her surname is a bit of a mouth full so she refers to herself as Clarissa B or just plain Clarissa, so please do the same. I'm sure you will all enjoy working with her. The second thing is that you all will have noticed by now that Geoff has not graced us with his presence this morning and the reason for that is because I've suspended him without pay pending further enquiries.

'Why what's he done now?' asked Ted.

'Normally I wouldn't say anything for confidential reasons and *The Advertiser* and *News and Mail* will probably have a field day with this so you may as well hear it from me first. Yesterday as you know I sent Geoff to Chobham to cover the farmers' market story. At six o'clock just after you'd all gone home I had a telephone call from a PC Gary Fenton from the Surrey Constabulary. They had received an emergency call from Brian Pembleton, landlord of the Castle Grove pub reporting a body in the cubicle of the gents' toilet. When the police and an ambulance arrived they removed the door only to find Geoff fast asleep on the loo. Not only has he broken our new no alcohol whilst on duty policy he has also brought the paper into serious disrepute. Mr Hackett has urged me to dismiss him immediately but I have to follow the correct procedures and I'm waiting for the company's solicitor to get back to me.

'Who will be picking up his work?' Ted asked.

'Clarissa will take over Jack's role and Jack will pick up all Geoff's work until further notice,' she said.

That amazed me because I didn't think I even had a role, which sort of made me laugh and feel angry at the same time.

'Clarissa still needs some initial training. She had her induction yesterday so knows what makes our newspaper tick, but Ted, I would like you to take her under your wing and show her the ropes, of course I will be here to assist as best I can myself,' she said.

It was the first time I had ever heard Nancy say that she would assist anyone which surprised me. Normally it's all delegation so that she can get away with doing practically nothing herself. Maybe Mr Hackett has rumbled her. I think Ted agrees.

Lisa offered to make us all a coffee, Clarissa had brought in her own fruit tea.

'Don't you worry, I always drink my own special tea, I'll do it myself,' she said.

Lisa smiled but I got the distinct impression that she was quite put out now that there was another young woman in the office.

Looking through Geoff's tray there isn't too much in the way of stories this week, just a flower show, a school reunion and an old lady's one hundredth birthday party. In his drawer I found some typed out templates. It looks like he uses the same phrases all the time and just changes the names, dates and locations depending on what kind of story he's covering. I think that's cheating but he seems to get away with it and he does have that reputation for padding things out. I wonder if he will get the sack. I also think that Clarissa may have been recruited by Mr Hackett and Nancy with that in mind. Ted said it's all a conspiracy. I think Lisa is hoping that Geoff won't come back; the others like Jasmine and Dan are quite dismissive of the whole situation. I know they can't stand Geoff!

15

This morning is the first time that I've taken my new prescription tablets and now I feel quite drowsy. There are fewer tablets now, no *valium* anymore and I'm very happy about that but I still have to take the other stuff, old man's tablets as Dr Brown calls them. I washed them all down with a pint of water complimented by a strong cup of coffee. Hopefully I will survive the day.

After last night's torrential rain everywhere is flooded. My train up to work from Farnham was nearly an hour late because part of the embankment had collapsed between Ash Vale and Brookwood, some trees are also down and there is chaos on the roads. Tony has gone out on his scooter down to Old Woking where the flooding is at its worst. For some reason he's taken two cameras with him. I'll have to ask him why when he gets back but I don't often see him.

We're still waiting to find out what's going to happen to Geoff. It's all gone very quiet but Ted seems to think that he'll get away with.

'Geoff will involve the union and he will get away with it if only on a technicality, you mark my word,' he said.

Lisa seems happier today. She's ditched her boyfriend although I really think that it's him who got rid of her which is why she was so upset the other day. Ted keeps telling me that now is my big chance to ask her out but I'm not interested. I'm not ready for a new relationship yet.

Apart from the floods and a couple of court cases not much is happening. I was hoping to go the court with Ted today but Nancy wants me to stay in the office in case any news comes in. Clarissa stayed as well and I've been showing her how to use the computer and the fiche. I told her about the time Geoff tried to send a letter from the fax.

'What happened?'

'He put the letter in an envelope, addressed it and then put a stamp on it,' I said.

'What's wrong with that?' she asked.

'Think about it!' I said.

I could see Lisa almost wetting herself in the background at which point Nancy appeared.

'Not more frivolity going on in my office?'

'No, I'm just showing Clarissa how to use the computer and other things,' I said.

Clarissa asked her how to use the fax.

'What's that?'

I couldn't believe that Nancy didn't know what it was so I pointed at it.

'Oh, you mean the facsimile machine.'

'Yes that's it.' I said.

Nancy then put her stern face on.

'I've been meaning to talk to you all about that. Last week I sent a message to Mr Hackett from that machine but his secretary never passed it on. Who changed the header?'

'Header?'

'Yes, the header. When it comes out at the other end it should read "from the *Woking Tribune*" but it doesn't,' she said.

I checked the settings and then realised what she was talking about.

'Oh, I see what you mean.'

'Yes, so who did that?'

'I don't know,' I said whilst trying not to laugh.

Someone had changed the header settings to 'Elmo Putney's Wine Bar,' probably Geoff before he got himself suspended. That's his kind of humour. I blamed him anyway because he wasn't here.

'Can you change it,' Nancy demanded.

'That's another nail in Geoffrey Bridger's coffin,' she said.

I felt really bad as I didn't really want to make things any worse for Geoff than what they were already!

After Nancy went back out Lisa came over and called me 'wicked'.

'It was probably him anyway,' I said.

On Saturday I've decided that I'll take a trip to the old Brookwood Asylum site or hospital as it's called now and have a proper look round. I want to see what it must have been like for Tommy all those years ago. Lisa said that a lot of the buildings have already been demolished but the chapel and clock-tower are still there.

'I think they're going to preserve those and some of the other bits,' she said.

I'm really looking forward to going there on Saturday now.

16

Today I took an extra long lunch break and went for a walk along the canal. The water level was quite low and the whole area smelt dank because of the heat. There were a lot of dead fish on the surface as well which didn't help. It wasn't very pleasant at all. Some men from the environmental health were there talking to a canal ranger. It was then that I realised I was actually on to a story.

'Good afternoon, I'm Jack Compton from the *Woking Tribune*, I was wondering if you chaps could tell me what's actually caused this problem.'

'Blimey, you got here quick mate, we've only just found out ourselves,' said the ranger.

'A narrowboat went through yesterday and its rudder got caught on a chain. The helmsman was able to release it and carry on. Unfortunately the chain was attached to an old drainage cover and this has caused the water level to drop.'

I didn't realise that boats could actually pass through this stretch of the canal. The ranger told me that navigation has only just been restored but there were still problems with inconsistent water levels caused by the lack of rain. I thought that was a bit strange, especially after all the flooding yesterday.

'We need days of rain if not weeks of it to keep the levels up,' he said.

One of the environmental health officers stated that they were arranging for contractors to come in and clear away all the dead fish.

'We need them to drain the whole pound completely and then replace the drain cover securely,' he said.

The ranger nodded. I thanked them for the chat, got all their names and then went back to the office to write up my story.

'That was a long lunch break,' said Nancy.

'Actually I got a story while I was out; I'm writing it up now. There's been a bit of an environmental problem on the Basingstoke Canal.'

'Oh well done, it's good to see someone being a bit pro-active at last,' she replied.

It seemed ironic that I should stumble on probably my biggest story so far simply by accident. At least now I might get to see my name in the paper even if it's not on the front page.

Lisa was sitting at her desk doing her nails again.

'Got nothing to do?' I quipped.

'Actually I've just finished typing up and copying all the new office policy documents, I'm taking a well deserved rest,' she said.

I noticed that there was a copy in my in-tray with a note saying 'please read then sign and return the yellow form on the back.

The form was addressed to Nancy and she needs to counter-sign it.

Lisa shouted over, 'make sure you sign it, I need to make another copy for your personal file afterwards.'

It all seemed very formal but it did make me realise that some changes were really starting to happen.

On the train home 'Side-Show' Mick, one of my old school friends who now also lives in Farnham told me that that there may be as many 250 unknown works by Picasso stored in the cellar of his grandfather's old house in Wrecclesham. I wondered if he's been taking too much LSD again but he does always make me laugh!

17

It's Saturday at last. The sun is out and there's not a cloud in the sky. I started the day with a bacon sandwich and a couple of coffees. Indeed the perfect start!

The train to Brookwood was only a couple of minutes late and then it took the twenty minutes to walk up to Knaphill from the station so all in all it hasn't taken me too long.

I arrived at the old asylum site and noticed that there is still a lot of demolition work going on, bulldozers, bonfires and massive piles of rubble where the rake of so-called progress is doing its deed. I walked past the new supermarket and DIY superstore across a newly laid car park. I used the clock-tower as my focal point. Parts of the hospital are still open and I could hear a woman singing *The Boys are Back in Town*, an old Eagles song quite loudly and there were patients being walked around the perimeters by the hospital staff.

Opposite the clock-tower there is a large hall, this must have been the Recreation Hall, further along is the chapel, inside it's mostly derelict with heaps of rubbish and upturned pews in the middle of the floor. I came to the morgue, a much smaller building with arch shaped windows. There is a black cross on either side of the chimney breast. I remember all these places being mentioned in Tommy's diaries. I then turned a corner and walked down a slight hill until I reached a small cottage with a slanted roof, there were two men cutting down trees, apple trees. Just then I heard a voice behind me.

'Young man, Jack isn't it?'

I looked around and there was a man perhaps in his mid-sixties towering over me. Because of the bright sunlight I couldn't see his face and the peak of his cap was hiding his eyes.

'You don't recognise me do you?' he said.

Just then he removed his cap and I remembered his squinty eyes. It was Mr Meredith. I hadn't seen him for a few years. He's the one who took the old tin over to Amanda. I was a bit surprised he recognised me.

'What brings you over here?' he asked.

I hesitated and then said, 'Well you really, I've come to find out more about Tommy.'

He laughed, 'Yes, it was some find that tin, I couldn't believe it when I opened it up and recognised the Compton family name on some of the letters. As you may remember I only live just round the corner from your aunt, we went to the same school together,' he said.

I told him that I had become infatuated with Tommy's life and was determined to find out more which was why I had come over to Knaphill.

'Come with me, I'll show you where the tin was found. See here, this is going be the road which leads to a lot more new houses; the tree in which the tin was discovered was felled close to where they're digging those new drains. I think they're going to call the road Percheron Drive; Percheron is the name of the breed of horses that used to be kept here.'

I found it all very interesting and it was fascinating to see the spot where the tree was located. Tommy would have had a great vantage point and would have been able to see over most of the hospital grounds.

'Come on, I'll show you some more,' Mr Meredith said.

He then took me along to a big water tower.

'Unfortunately this has got to come down too, we've got to create a new reservoir down by the canal so all the water has somewhere to go. There's near on 3,000 gallons in there and beneath the tower is a sunken well which is 880 feet deep and that will have to be filled in with aggregates,' he said.

I thought it was such a shame that the tower had to be demolished as you could probably see most of Woking and beyond from up there. Mr Meredith agreed but told me that part of the structure was unsafe.

He then took me over towards a road called the Broadway and showed me where the pig farm used to be. I remember that Tommy had worked there; he speaks of it in his diaries with some affection.

'Right young Jack, if you want to know more about this place I suggest you speak to Philip Janner, he's a local historian, he's always sniffing around and what he doesn't know about the Woking area, no-one knows. He normally drinks up the road in The Crown pub, just ask for him in there,' he said.

I thanked Mr Meredith for his time. I couldn't believe I was lucky enough to bump into him, he has been such a great help but I forgot to ask him why some of the pages had been removed from Tommy's diaries. Shit!

I looked at my watch and realised that The Crown would now be open. After all this walking and excitement I thought I could do with a pint. In the pub there was an old lady behind the bar. She didn't look very friendly. White hair, glasses and bright blue nail varnish.

'What do you want?' she snarled.

'Err, a pint of cider please.'

'What cider?'

'That cider…'

'We only sell one cider,' she said and chuckled.

'I haven't seen you in here before.'

'No, just passing through really,' I said.

The pub was empty except for a man with long ginger hair and a beard who was sitting in the corner. It looked like he was picking out his horses from the paper.

'Excuse me; do you happen to know someone called Phillip Janner who drinks in here?' I asked.

The woman behind the bar looked surprised. 'Know him? Everybody knows the silly old fart, he's always in here. What do you want with him?'

'I'm trying to find out a bit more about the old asylum, you know, Brookwood Hospital and I've been told he may be able to help.'

'Oh yes, he knows everything, his father used to be an attendant over there after he had finished working on the railway, I remember him actually, he was always telling us horrible stories about the place. Old Janner normally comes in during the early part of the evening. He lives down the Broadway, No 34, give him a knock; he's usually at home this time of day.'

I thanked her and was happy to leave. I felt like I had just been chewed over by a Rottweiler. I walked down the Broadway and eventually found Mr Janner's house. There were a lot of garden gnomes and some ornamental stone frogs in the front garden outside by the porch. I knocked on the front door but there was no answer. I was just about to walk away when a man came round from a side entrance.

'Can I help you young man?'

'Yes, I'm looking for a Mr Phillip Janner.'

'... and what would you want with him?'

'I've heard he knows quite a lot about Brookwood Hospital.'

'Ah, that's alright then, I'm Phil Janner,' he said.

He invited me around the back of the house into the kitchen where he was in the middle of eating a Cornish pasty.

'Let me finish this and then you can fire away,' he said.

I told him that I was the grandson of Tommy Compton and that I was trying to find out more about his life, particularly his time at the old asylum.

'I remember a lot of the staff over there but unfortunately your man was a bit before my time, there's a lady who lives down in Oak Tree Road and she keeps a record of everything that went on in there. She was married to one of the farmhands but he got killed during the war. She's about ninety years old now but she's still got her faculties about her and she loves talking about the place.'

'What's her name?' I asked.

'Everyone calls her Missy but her real name is Hope Pengelley,' he said.

I thanked Mr Janner for his time and promised to call on him again; Oak Tree Road is on my route back to the train station so I thought I would call in on the way. Mr Janner couldn't remember the number of the house but he told me that it's the one with the green door and all the yellow rose bushes outside.

I knocked.

'Come in!' a voice shouted.

The door was on the latch so I poked my head around; there was a lady in the hallway sitting in a wheelchair.

'Are you Jack?' she asked.

'Yes, how do you know?'

'Phil Janner just rung and said that you might be popping by.'

'Cup of tea?'

'No thanks, I haven't got long, I have a train soon,' I replied.

'So you're Jack Compton, I know all about your grandfather, I knew him well. He was at my wedding you know.'

I felt myself going cold and my arms filled up with goose pimples.

'Tommy and my Donald were inseparable; they worked at the farm over the road and then eventually went into the RAF together at the start of the war. Tommy was Don's navigator when they got shot down in Malta.'

I felt a bit uneasy as I guessed what she was going to tell me next.

'I'm glad your grandfather got out, he went on to have a marvellous life. If I was going to lose my Don during the war, I'm glad it was Tommy who was with him during his final moments,' she said.

'Your grandfather was a lovely man, he should never have been in the asylum in the first place, he suffered so much abuse, Don and his mother felt sorry for him and took him in. It was such a shame about Maisie too. He doted on her.'

'Maisie?'

'Yes Maisie, it was a forbidden love affair. Patients were not allowed to court each other but those two young lovers found a way. It was beautiful but it ended so tragically. It was like Romeo and Juliet. There was a misunderstanding and Maisie apparently thought that Tommy had left without saying goodbye, he hadn't. She managed to get out one evening just before dusk and got hit by a train, killed instantly. Tommy was distraught, I thought he would never recover, perhaps he never did.'

I felt myself becoming tearful. Mrs Pengelley noticed and offered me a tissue.

'What happened after that?'

'A few weeks later Tommy told us that he was just going to walk out of the place. I think he had some inside help, there was a lady called Mrs Skilton and I think it was her who took him in shortly after he absconded.'

I told Mrs Pengelley that I knew Tommy had married someone called Katherine from the asylum.

'Yes, that was Maisie's friend. I think that she really wanted to look after Tommy on Maisie's behalf. She knew that Maisie was the only one in Tommy's heart but she had a good heart too and was another one who should never have been in the asylum. Do you know what happened to her?' she asked.

'My Aunt Amanda told me that she died from tuberculosis in 1949. She's buried out in Malta.' I said.

'Oh dear, how sad,' she sniffled.

I thanked Mrs Pengelley for her time and accepted her invitation to visit her again one day.

Today has been an important experience for me and I found out quite a lot. The lady also confirmed that Tommy was a navigator in the RAF and not a pilot as Amanda thought. Perhaps I need to go home and write some things down so I can keep everything in perspective. It's been very exciting talking to someone who actually remembers my grandfather during his time at the asylum, something I shall never forget. I must tell Amanda.

18

Monday mornings are usually dour but this one was always going to be different. On arrival Ted told me to 'Shush!' He was loitering close to Nancy's office door.

'Geoff's in there and there's already been some raised voices,' he whispered.

Lisa was making the coffees and Dan was in the office which was unusual, particularly at this time of the week.

'Just a flying visit, I just needed to pick up some stationary, I'm covering the cricket at Guildford later,' he said.

Lisa told me that Jasmine had been in earlier as well. We don't see her or Dan until at least a Wednesday afternoon so it was all a bit odd.

'They're just vultures waiting for the kill,' said Ted.

'What do you mean?'

'The Geoff thing, they're waiting to see if he'll get the sack but he's been in there well over an hour already.'

Just then Nancy appeared.

'Good morning everyone, I hope you all had a nice weekend.'

For some reason she looked over in my direction and smiled which made me feel a bit peculiar.

'As you may be aware I've had Mr Bridger in the office with me this morning and no doubt you'll all be wondering what's been going on. I have agreed that he can return to his desk from tomorrow but he will be restricted to office duties only. I have also removed him from the weekend on-call rota which will mean that Clarissa will take Geoff's place until further notice. Does anybody have any questions?'

'Why have you allowed him to come back?' Lisa asked.

'That's strictly confidential.'

'Will I still have to pick up his work?' I interrupted.

'Yes, but Geoff can assist you from here when appropriate.'

'So what office work will he be doing?' asked Lisa.

Nancy hesitated. 'I'm not sure just yet, I'll have to work out some kind of plan,' she said.

'He can always make the teas and coffees,' Lisa joked.
Everyone laughed.

'Look this is serious; you all need to get to grips with what you're doing. Don't forget I am trying to steer a steady and professional ship here,' Nancy shouted.

'*In the Navy, in the Navy,*' sang Ted.

'... and Ted you of all people should know better.'

I could see that Nancy was starting to lose her temper. She must have realised it too and walked back into her office. Now everyone was speculating about what had happened to Geoff.

'Did you notice that she let him out through the fire exit, there was some smarmy looking union bloke with him,' said Ted.

'I noticed that as well, I reckon he's got off on a technicality and I think I know why,' said Lisa.

'What technicality?' I asked.

'Well those new office policy documents I typed out last week, he wouldn't have received his copy in time. I bet the union guy has picked up on that.'

'That's a fair point, I haven't signed mine yet. Nancy may have needed the signed form on his file to be able to get him hook, line and sinker,' said Ted.

'But he's brought the newspaper into disrepute; wouldn't that be a case for instant dismissal anyway?' I asked.

'I'm not sure who the union bloke was but they can be very clever. They have a knack of turning things back in favour of the employee. He would have found a loophole somewhere and that's how Geoff has probably got off. Don't forget that he's restricted to office duties now so some kind of punishment has been handed out somewhere, probably a final warning,' said Ted.

I was quite impressed with the way Lisa was thinking things through. It was clever how she picked up on the fact that there may have been a 'technicality' as she put it. Of course she may not be right but something tells me that she's probably hit the nail on the head and Ted agrees.

'She'll be our editor soon at this rate,' he said.

This afternoon I had my first court story. There's been an 'ice cream war' between two vendors, Carlos and Pedro. Pedro has been encroaching on Carlos' patch and they ended up having a punch up in front of a load of little kids over in St John's. Both have been bound over to keep the peace and they were each fined £100 by the magistrate.

'Girls and boys come out to play; the ice cream shark is on his way...'

I laugh but I'm still waiting for that big one, a story that I can really get my teeth into. It's about time that I saw my name in lights, I need a scoop!

19

Its Geoff's first day back in the office after his suspension. He's been very quiet and subdued. I get the impression that Lisa has been dying to ask him some questions but hopefully she's thought better of it and has kept herself to herself for once. Nancy has given Geoff some archive material that she wants transferred on to the new computers and Beryl has come in especially to assist.

'Everything that is stored on the fiche needs to go on to disk so that we can access it all through our new software.' Nancy told us.

There's an IT man in the LAN Room setting up a new server which apparently has cost Mr Hackett thousands of pounds.

I don't think Nancy really understands what's going on. Mr Hackett has been in and had to tell her that IT stood for 'Information Technology' which was quite amusing. It also seems strange to see Geoff wearing a tie and I noticed that it's one from the box which Mr Hackett brought in one day last week.

Ted has just come back from his old stomping ground in Maybury. Some mad guy has been running around the streets in just his shorts wielding a samurai sword and threatening the residents although I don't think anyone has been hurt. It appears his wife had been having an affair with a next door neighbour and he went on the rampage.

'I'm going to have fun writing this one up later,' he said.

This afternoon Geoff was scouring through all the old articles on the fiche.

'You lot want to read some of these stories, there's some good ones on here,' said Geoff.

We all huddled over behind his chair to look at the screen.

Canal woman fined for infanticide after throwing her baby into the Basingstoke Canal at St John's in 1925.

Pirbright juvenile sentenced to three years prison after shooting his foster mother dead with five shots from a pistol in 1958.

'Nothing like that happens around here anymore does it,' said Lisa.

'Unfortunately not, but it's nice when the odd juicy story does come along,' said Ted.

'What, even a murder?' Lisa asked.

'Sadly, yes, even a murder and we haven't had one of those in Woking for awhile.'

'Just as well,' said Nancy as she suddenly appeared behind us.

'So is there any chance that any of you are going to do some work for me today?'

We all gradually retreated back to our own desks.

'Actually, it's a good learning session for the young ones, they need to know a bit about the history of the paper and what used to go on in the area,' said Ted.

'Just get on with your work and find me some new stories, we're a bit light on any fresh news this week,' moaned Nancy as she went back into her office.

'We weren't being that loud were we?' asked Lisa looking quite concerned.

'No, it's just the old girl being nosey,' said Geoff.

'Do you mind not using that phrase, I'm twenty years older than Nancy, God only knows what you all must call me behind my back,' said Beryl.

We all laughed and Geoff actually apologised.

Clarissa just sat there saying nothing as usual.

Lisa went out to make the coffees.

'Hey Jack, look she's got that short skirt on again!' said Ted with a wink.

'Behave yourself you disgusting old man,' screamed Beryl.

Ted looked embarrassed.

'Yes, don't forget, we now have a new code of practice in the office,' quipped Geoff.

'Oh what irony again,' I thought.

I was just looking at the clock and was thinking about going home when Nancy called me into her office.

'How are you Jack?'

'Okay, I think.'

'Only Okay?'

'No I'm fine actually.'

'What have I told you before about being positive?'
I began to worry.
You've been back two or three weeks now; I just want to find out how you are.'
'I'm fine, really, thank you.'
'Are you sure?'
'Yes, I am.'
'How do you think you've been getting on with your work?'
'Okay, I think, err, sorry, I meant to say that I'm happy that I've got a few stories under my belt now,' I said.
'Which one has given you the most satisfaction so far?'
'I would say the one about canal, its low water level and pollution.
'Why's that?'
'I stumbled on the story by accident and everything just fell into place. It was a good story to write up.'
'Yes it probably is your best article since you've been back however I'd like to see a bit more substance and originality next time.'
'You're writing is too much like Geoff's and I think you're capable of much better things and I know your best work is still yet to come,' she added.
I nodded and agreed and then told her that I hoped to get a front page story soon.
'Your time will come,' she said.
By now I was hoping that she had finished with me so that I could go home but then she started asking lots more questions.
'Have you seen anything of Kazkia lately?'
'Err no, ever since I told her that I couldn't wait for a divorce she's been avoiding me,' I said.
'How long have you two been apart now?'
'About six months.'
'So on what grounds are you hoping to get divorced, adultery, unreasonable behaviour or just the two year separation thing?'
'I have grounds for adultery and unreasonable behaviour but I think I'll just wait for a two year separation. I'm in no hurry,' I said.
'No, you don't want to rush into anything new just yet.'

I felt uncomfortable with all her questions and got the distinct impression there was more to come and that there was a reason behind what felt like an interrogation.

'Do you think my marriage break up is still affecting my work?' I asked.

'No, I'm more concerned about other distractions.'

'What other distractions?'

'A little bird tells me that you fancy Lisa, am I right?'

'Actually no, we get on alright as friends but I don't fancy her, she's far too young and I don't think we have that much in common.'

'Well you know that office relationships are frowned upon here don't you!'

I couldn't believe what I was hearing after what Nancy had done to me the other week.

'I know what you're thinking,' she said.

'A woman my age has needs and I just love young men, lots of them but if you did go out with Lisa that would mean that I couldn't have you again.'

I shuddered and felt physically sick, almost frightened but then she smiled.

'I'm only playing with you, I've got my husband back and I'm happy again so your safe now, at least for awhile but I would appreciate your utmost discretion,' she said with a slight look of concern.

She must have sensed my relief.

'Just go out and find me that big story,' she said.

I left her office feeling quite perplexed and uneasy but something told me that maybe, just maybe, a big story is just around the corner.

20

After all the furore of my conversation with Nancy yesterday I needed to treat myself to a change of scenery and a couple of stiff drinks. I decided to pop over to Camberley and visit one of the old haunts from my teenage years, The Four Horse Shoes in Frimley Road. The pub was nearly empty but the lady behind the bar seemed to recognise me.

'You're the Compton boy, Jack isn't it?' she said.

'Err yes,' I said feeling quite surprised.

'I remember your dad, such a lovely man.'

Her comment totally knocked me back and I felt shocked and of course very intrigued. I wondered what she was going to say next.

'It's a shame what happened to him. He was cute, a bit of a ladies' man but everyone loved him especially the women. I don't know how your mother coped, well actually I do, it's so sad that she was also driven to an early grave because of it all, about 1970 wasn't it?'

I nodded, 'Yes, I think it was, when I was four,' I said.

I got the impression that she just assumed that I knew everything so I just let her carry on talking.

'What do you remember about it all?' I asked.

'Oh your father, very hippyish but he was also a good looking lad, definitely a ladies' man. I remember young girls falling to their knees and almost kissing his feet,' she said with a laugh.

'If you don't mind me asking, what's your name?'

I felt obliged to ask.

'I'm Mary, Mary née Hutton; I used to work with your mum Rachel down at the book binding factory until she got the sack. I remember the day she came in a bit high on something and told us about it all. There was no mercy from employers in those days and she was fired in an instant. It was a dangerous place to work, there was a lot of heavy machinery and you had to keep your wits about you down there,' she said.

'What happened after that?'

'When she was in the family way with you she found out that your dad had got another woman pregnant at about the same time. He chose to be with her instead and left your mum on her own to cope. In the end it tipped her over the edge. She was in a very bad way and it turned her to drink, well, much more than drink. When she died, she was just a shadow of the person she used to be, it was such a shame, she was such a pretty thing,' she said.

I noticed that Mary had then realised that I was beginning to feel uneasy.

'Sorry if this is all bringing the memories back and upsetting you,' she said.

'It's not. Obviously I never knew my father and I can hardly remember my mother at all. What you're telling me is all very new to me, all I know about my past is what my Aunt Amanda has told me,' I confided.

'Amanda oh yes, what a kind and loving woman. She took you in and looked after you as if you were her own, I still see her about sometimes, but not often.'

I felt compelled to ask. 'What happened to my father?'

'Don't you know?'

'No. I've never really been told.'

'He was killed in a car crash in Epsom, a few weeks before you were born. He had gone with two friends to watch the horse racing and their car hit a lamp post on the way back. The other two were killed instantly and your father died a few days later at the hospital in Wimbledon.'

I told Mary that my family didn't really talk about him but I knew my grandfather had come over from Malta for his funeral in 1966.

'Yes, I remember your grandfather coming over. It was all very awkward at the time. The other woman came to the funeral. Both women were heavily pregnant and there was some kind of stand-off between them. Your Aunt Amanda was mortified but acted as an intermediary if I remember.'

'I need to confirm, was my father's Christian name Lionel?'

'Yes, of course, I can't believe that you don't already know,' she said.

I sort of knew it was but I just needed to make sure that we were definitely talking about the same person. It was then that I remembered that Tommy talks of a Lionel in at least one of his diaries. Lionel Breavman if I remember correctly. I think he was his best friend at the asylum. Perhaps it's him who my father was named after. I then asked Mary how she recognised me.

'When I was in my teens I used to babysit for your aunt when you were a little boy, right up until you were about five years old. I have never forgotten those big brown eyes of yours,' she said.

I smiled. Just as I was about to leave, Mary pulled me back.

'Have you ever met your sister?'

'Sister?'

'Yes your sister, well your half sister really.'

'Err; no I didn't know I had one.' I said.

'Well you have and her name is Jayne.'

'Remember that your father managed to get two women pregnant at the same time. Your mother of course was one and Jayne is the result of the other pregnancy,' she said.

I hadn't even thought of that and I felt a bit stupid for not thinking straight.

'Jayne Compton?' I asked.

'No, Jayne O'Leary. Her mother was Laura and her stepfather was called Jack, his nickname was Big Jack!'

I remember seeing that Tommy had used the O'Leary name when he joined the army shortly after absconding from the asylum. There must be a connection somewhere I thought. Now I was confused.

On the way back home I felt drained, absolutely exhausted, completely flabbergasted by the day's events. Now I feel that I must find my sister as a matter of priority. I wonder if she actually knows about me.

21

It was very quiet in the office this morning. Geoff had phoned in sick and all the others were out so it was just me and Lisa. I decided to tell her about my little trip to Camberley last night. I somehow had to get things off my chest and I knew that she would listen.

'It must be terrible growing up without a father,' she said.

'Yes, and my mother died when I was little, it was my aunt who brought me up.'

She kept saying how sad everything was, it all felt very patronising but I knew she meant well. I told her that my grandfather was once a patient at Brookwood Hospital.

'Oh my great-grandfather Cyril used to work there, he was the farm bailiff, he lived in a house called Almond Villa by the North Gate, it's used as a half way house for people who are leaving care and going back into the community these days,' she said.

'When was your great-grandfather there?'

'He had been there since the 1920s right up until he died in 1956, my dad used to tell me lots of stories about him and my grandfather. My grandfather worked there just after the war but didn't feel comfortable having to mix with all the patients so he left just after a couple of months,' she said.

Lisa then started asking more questions about my background which at first was quite uncomfortable. I told her that I had just found out about my father and the real reason no-one spoke of him.

'Oh that's terrible, what your poor mother must have gone through,' she said.

I agreed. It's all been very difficult and I felt very selfish because up until last night I didn't really know anything about my parents. It took a woman who I didn't really know to tell me the truth about everything. Even though I love Amanda very much she has never told me much about my father and I've always sort of despised her for that. Lisa reached for my hand. At that point Nancy suddenly appeared.

'Hello, hello, what's going on here?' she asked.

'Nothing, absolutely nothing,' I snapped.

'It doesn't look like that to me,' said Nancy.

'Jack was just telling me his life story and I was reaching out to console him,' said Lisa.

'Yeah, right, pull the other one,' said Nancy as she went back into her office.

I just looked at Lisa and we both laughed. Now I wonder if some of the chit-chat we've had is giving out the wrong signals. I hope she doesn't think that I'm making a move for her. Yes, she is very pretty but I'm not ready to be with anyone else yet. I'm not ready for all that hurt again if things go wrong. I decided to tell Lisa what I was thinking.

'Lisa, I hope you don't think that I'm trying to chat you up when we have these quiet moments in the office,' I confided.

'Of course not, but it would be nice if you were,' she said with a little chuckle.

I felt myself blush.

'I'm not ready for anyone new yet, I'm still recovering from my last relationship,' I said.

'Who Nancy?' Lisa joked.

'No Kazkia of course.'

Lisa laughed.

'I wouldn't go out with you anyway, it would spoil our friendship and besides, I fancy a boy down in Brookwood who works for Wesson's.

'Wesson's?'

'Yes, Wesson's the fencing company.'

I actually felt quite disappointed when she told me that, maybe I do fancy her but probably haven't noticed because of all the other crap which has been going on with my life just recently.

Just then Nancy came back into the office.

'I hope you two have finished making love in work time,' she said.

Lisa and I just looked at each other and smiled.

'I've just had Clarissa in my office and she's decided to leave us with immediate effect, so Jack, I want you to take back her work until I can find someone to fill her shoes. I will be advertising for a new junior reporter in next week's jobs section.'

'Can I apply for that?' Lisa asked.

'You're our secretary. Remember, you need to be here for at least six months before you can apply for another position, I need you to carry on doing what you're doing and when you're not idling your hours away talking to Jack and the others you do a very good job,' she said quite abruptly.

Lisa looked stunned.

'But it's not fair if you can bring someone in off the street and they get the job ahead of me,' she said.

'That's a fair point,' I said.

'I'll think about it, but Lisa you really need to read your contract of employment, it states everything quite clearly in there,' Nancy retorted.

After Nancy left the office again I told Lisa what Ted had said.

'What did he say?'

'The other day he said that you would be our editor soon.'

Lisa laughed. At least that put a smile back on her face. She then asked if I knew that Geoff was thinking of leaving the *Tribune*.

I didn't.

'Do you think he'll really leave?' she asked.

'I'm not sure but I know he liked his freedom and that has all been taken away from him. He no longer has that opportunity to grab himself a crafty pint when he's out and about. He probably challenged the discipline situation because he wanted to leave with a good reference,' I said.

'But they're not allowed to give a bad reference, are they?' Lisa asked.

'I don't think so but if they gave no reference at all that would be quite negative as well.'

Lisa told me she'd heard that Geoff had been hoping for a job at the *Woking Informer* and that's why he'd phoned in sick.

'I think he's gone for an interview today,' she said.

Even they wouldn't take him on I thought.

She laughed. I think she knew what I was thinking!

22

Sometimes I wonder about Lisa. Does she mean what she says or is what she's trying to say just some kind of Freudian slip? It actually happens quite a lot. Her conversation with Geoff this morning was a peach!

'Good Morning, Geoff,' she said when he appeared in the office.

'Hello, young lady,' he replied.

'How was your interview yesterday?' she asked.

'Very good, thank you.'

Geoff looked aghast while Lisa smiled. He'd just been rumbled and started to look angry.

'Oh, sorry, I got a bit confused, I forgot you were off sick, silly me, are you feeling better now?'

Geoff just growled like he normally does.

'I'm feeling much better now and I suggest you mind your own business young lady,' he snapped.

'What's my business; is not your business,' he added rather sharply.

Lisa looked down into her paperwork and just smiled. I could sense the rage in Geoff and was waiting for him to explode but just then Nancy walked in.

'Good morning everyone, like I've already said, I'm advertising Clarissa's post so if you know anyone who may be interested please point them in my direction.'

'What about me?' Lisa asked.

'Put an application form in and then we'll see,' Nancy replied.

Nancy went back into the office and then Geoff began to question Lisa about her aspirations.

'What makes you think you can become a newspaper reporter?'

'Because I can, I listen to you guys and I want to do the same, I think I can do what you do, I'm good at adapting to different things quite quickly.'

'It takes years to become a good reporter,' said Geoff.

'But you're not a good reporter are you?' Lisa replied.

'What the hell do you mean?'

'Jack showed me the templates you use when you write up all the mundane stuff, basically you just cheat and I can do much, much better than that.'

I felt myself sinking into my chair and felt rather embarrassed that Lisa had implicated me in the conversation. I then noticed Geoff was looking daggers in my direction.

'What have you been saying to this young floozy?' he asked.

'Nothing, absolutely nothing,' I replied.

I knew I was being a bit economical with the truth and felt very uncomfortable. I could see Lisa winking at me and trying to roll her eyes at the same time.

Just then Geoff stood up; his frown was more accentuated than usual.

'There are only two proper reporters in this newspaper office and that's me and Ted, just remember that,' he shouted.

'Actually if you're using templates and you're not allowed out of the office anymore, how can you be a proper reporter? Anyway, Ted thinks that I'm good enough to be your editor soon.' Lisa retorted.

I was trying not to laugh but also felt that this was another conversation where Geoff would explode and I didn't want to see Lisa collapsing in tears again so I decided to intervene.

'Lisa, two sugars please,' I said.

'Yes, go and make the coffee, that's obviously what you do best,' said Geoff.

'Fuck you; fuck both of you,' screamed Lisa.

She turned around and walked straight into Nancy's office without knocking. About five minutes later they both came out.

'Okay, Lisa go back to your desk and finish typing that document for me, you two, in my office now!' Nancy demanded.

Geoff and I looked at each other, got up and walked into her office.

'Call yourself grown men? Young Lisa has more metal than both of you put together, man up the pair of you and start treating that young lady with respect. I'm not standing for any more of this and Geoff, remember that you're on a final warning. Lisa has just told me about your flirtation with the *Informer* yesterday when you were supposed to be off sick. Well you won't get a reference off me and if it wasn't for Clarissa leaving I would sack you on the spot right now.'

Geoff shrugged his shoulders and looked really embarrassed. I could hear him muttering something under his breath but couldn't make out what he was saying.

'Get out of my office now, the pair of you,' Nancy screamed.

I was actually quite annoyed that I'd been dragged into it all and my perception of Lisa had changed rather quickly. Any respect I had for her was diminishing by the second.

'Two-faced cow,' I thought.

Back home I thought about my day. Morale in the office is low and I have seen Lisa in a different light this afternoon. She seems to be one of those people who let you into their confidence and then cuts you loose when it suits. It's all 'Me, me, me' with her and I find that very disappointing. When I first met her I thought she was a really nice person but now I'm not so sure. Geoff's attitude doesn't help either and now that he's been condemned to the office for the whole of his working day he just sits and snarls with a massive chip on his shoulder.

This evening I've found a short letter dated 18th May 1966 that Tommy had received from my father. It was tucked away in the back of one of his diaries which Amanda was sent from Malta shortly after he died.

Dear Father,

I'm trusting that this letter finds you well and that you are still enjoying the Maltese sunshine.

Amanda has told me that you are very disappointed to hear of my recent indiscretion. I would like to apologise to all concerned. I know that I should not have let this happen and that I have upset and shamed everyone. If you were here I would have asked for your advice. Again, I am very, very sorry.

Both girls have decided to keep their babies and they are due to be born around the same time. I don't really know what to do but I

have decided to leave Rachel for Laura and I will be living with her in Mychett in the flat above the butcher's shop.
I will write to you again when I am settled.

Please forgive me, your loving son

Lionel

The discovery of the letter which was written just before my father was killed has shocked me but it confirms some of the things that Mary at the Four Horse Shoes told me the other day. Despite his indiscretion I can feel some kind of warmth towards him. His apology alone seems sincere and it's the only evidence that I have ever seen of his existence. I may find out more about him if I can track down Jayne. I now think about her all the time and what she must be like. I wonder if she knows that she has a brother, I wonder if she knows about me!

23

Today has been another crazy day. Lisa came into the office at eleven o'clock after taking her driving test. She had failed. It was her third time and Geoff was trying not to wind her up but he kept saying 'mind the traffic' each time she got up to make the coffee. I thought there was going to be another war of words but fortunately nothing happened. Nancy has been having her office walls painted today so she was sat out with us at Beryl's desk, perhaps that why Geoff was more conscious of keeping his views to himself for once. Ted has been working with a reporter from the *Daily Express* who is doing a feature on Brookwood Cemetery and its connection with the railway during the war. Nancy's been rubbing her hands together.

'All good money for the *Tribune* and brownie points for me,' she said.

I laughed.

Just after that Mr Hackett came in and I later overheard him talking to Nancy about a drop in circulation figures and advertising revenue. Nancy looked concerned. He's called a meeting with his partners in London in two weeks time and he wants Nancy to attend but it clashes with her holiday, she has two weeks booked up on Hydra, one of the Greek islands and now she may have to cancel.

'Surely Mr Hackett will understand,' Lisa intimated.

'I doubt that, if I have to cancel, I have to cancel, my job comes first; it means the world to me.'

I actually felt sorry for Nancy and I could sense that she was trying to fight back tears. Geoff just made himself scarce for a few minutes, women's tears are not his thing and I couldn't imagine him getting involved in that kind of conversation.

After lunch I was in the office alone so I spent some time looking through all the local directories trying to find any record of my sister. Lots of O'Leary's but no Jayne O'Leary's. I then decided to look up butcher's shops in Mychett going back to the 1960s but the only one I could find had gone and was now a bicycle shop. I remembered from my father's letter to Tommy that he had moved into the flat above so decided to phone the bicycle shop to see if they knew anything.

'Hello, is that the owner?'

'Hang on…' said a voice.

I could then hear some whispers in the background until another person came to the phone.

'Hello this is Chris Mason, I'm the manager. How can I help you?'

'Err hello, I'm Jack Compton from the *Woking Tribune*; I'm trying to trace a Jayne O'Leary who lived above your shop probably back in the 1960s or 70s. Her mother was called Laura.'

'Sorry, I don't know anyone by that name, I've been here for over twenty-five years now and I'm sure I would have heard of them if they'd been living upstairs,' he said.

'Okay, thanks, can I give you my number in case you do remember anything,'

'Of course, Oh hang on a minute, there was a Jayne upstairs, I think her mother's dead now, is the Jayne you're looking for spelt with a "y" as in J.A.Y.N.E,' he asked.

'Yes.'

'There was a Jayne living up there until about ten years ago, she got married again, she's got a couple of kids, two boys I think.'

'Do you remember her surname?'

'Wait, I'm just trying to think. Well I don't know what it is now but when she lived upstairs it would have been Rogers, that's it, Jayne Rogers she was married to Mark, the postmaster's son.'

'Is he still about?' I asked.

'No, he's long gone I'm afraid, he drowned in a swimming accident in the River Wey near Guildford some years ago. Sorry I can't help you any further, if I think of anything I'll give you a ring, what's your number?'

'0483 765048,' I said.

'If I find out anything, I'll give you a ring, what's your name again?'

'Jack, Jack Compton.' I thanked him for his time and leant back in the chair as I put the phone down.

I was left wondering and then spent the next few minutes just gazing out of the window and watching the raindrops getting heavier and heavier. I was just about to call it a day and skive off early when the phone rang.

'Is that Jack?'

'Yes, Jack Compton here,' I said.

'Hello mate, this is Chris from Mason's in Mychett, the bike shop, you phoned me earlier and asked about a lady called Jayne.'

'Yes that's right, I did.'

'Well just after speaking to you an old bloke called Bert who's lived here for donkeys' years came into the shop and I asked him if he remembered her at all. He did, she had moved to Worsley Road in Frimley Green with her mum Laura and a fat bloke called Big Jack in the early 1970s. Her mum died in the late eighties I think. He remembered Jayne getting married again in 1990. Her surname is Smith now and she's living up in Woking with her new husband. He doesn't know exactly where she lives but he does know that she works in a bakers, Heater's, I think he said it was called.'

'I know the shop well, it's not far from my office, that's a great help,' I said.

After I put the phone down I looked at my watch. I wondered if the Jack he mentioned was the same one that Amanda and Mary had both told me about. I was going to catch the 15:55 train home but decided to pop around to the bakers to see if it was still open. Just as I got there a big black lady was turning the lights off and was about to put up the 'closed' sign. I managed to get her attention.

'Can I help you?' she asked.

'Yes please, I'm looking for Jayne, err Jayne Smith, does she work here?'

'Peroxide Jayne, yes she's still here but only works in the mornings, finishes at two so she can go and pick her kids up from school. What do you want with her, she's married and I know it's not to you?'

'If she's the Jayne I'm looking for, then I'm her brother. Does she spell her name with a "y" as in J.A.Y.N.E?' I asked.

'Yes she does.'

'That's great,' I said.

'Hang on; you wouldn't be Jack by any chance would you?'

'Yes, I'm Jack, Jack Compton.'

'Well blow me down with a feather. She was only talking about you this morning, about the brother she's never met, she's been looking you for years but no-one would tell her anything. Her dad died in a car crash in 1966 and it was only when her mother Laura passed away a few years ago that she found out about you, your dad was Lionel wasn't it?'

Yes, yes it was,' I said rather excitedly.

This confirmed all I needed to know. I had almost found my sister.

I thanked the lady and asked if Jayne would be at work tomorrow.

'Oh yes eight o'clock she starts, Dave her husband takes the boys to school and as I said, she leaves at two to pick them up.'

This is the second time now that a complete stranger has given me information about my family. This is wonderful news but I'm not sure if I should tell Amanda.

24

I couldn't wait to get out of bed and make my way to work this morning. I caught the earlier train so that I could go to the bakers shop and introduce myself to Jayne. I'm assuming the lady from yesterday would have told her that I was looking for her. I seemed to remember a girl with dyed blond hair serving me there a few months ago and I'm now wondering if it's actually the same person. I feel quite nervous about meeting her but I'm glad to know that she's been trying to find me as well.

When I got to the shop there was a big burly guy behind the counter.

'Yes mush, what you after?' he asked.

'I've come to see Jayne,' I replied rather nervously.

'Jayne, JAYNE, get your fucking ass down 'ere there's some geezer wanting to talk to you,' he shouted.

About a minute later, the door behind the counter opened slowly and a face appeared. It was Jayne, her hair was tied back and she was wearing glasses.

'You must be Jack, Doris told me that you might come and see me this morning. We have so much to talk about. I'll take an early break, let's go for a walk.'

We ended up on a bench in Woking Park. Everything felt quite surreal and almost as if nothing at all was happening. I just kept looking down at the bright flowers in the flowerbed and I was feeling rather shy but knowing that I shouldn't. This was my half-sister and neither of us was to blame for the situation we found ourselves in.

'So you met Doris yesterday,' she said.

'Yes, I had a telephone conversation with a man called Chris Mason who manages the bike shop in Mychett. He managed to find out a couple of things, rang me back and here we are,' I said.

'Yes, the bike shop, I lived there with my mum Laura when it was still a butchers, it used to sell everything, even free range eggs. We moved along the road to Frimley Green when I was five. Big Jack had a two bedroom house so it made sense. Big Jack had always been about; he went to school with my mum and yours I think. He always spoke of your mum with affection so I wondered if they once had something going on.'

'What do you know about our dad?' I asked.

'Not much. I've heard him described as a loveable rogue, a bit of a ladies' man and all that. He died just before I was born you know.'

'Yes I know. I was told the same story but no-one really spoke of him. The day of his funeral has been mentioned a few times and that's about it. The only other thing I know is from a letter I found which he had written to his father, our grandfather Tommy.'

I showed Jayne the letter which I had decided to take with me. She started to cry and we began to hug each other, it was all very emotional but somehow I felt that I had already known Jayne all my life. In reality, I've only known she's existed for a few days.

'He was very naughty getting two women pregnant at the same time,' she said.

'What's your actual birthday?' I asked.

'30th July 1966.'

'Same as mine, exactly the same day as me, that means we were both born on the day England won the World Cup!'

She laughed.

'I hate football.'

'Do you think that he had sex with both our mums on the same day?' she asked.

'It's possible considering that we were both born on the same day but it doesn't always work that way, or does it?'

'I don't know and I've always wondered if my step dad Big Jack was involved somehow. It's funny that you're called Jack as well.'

'Yes, I've been wondering that. If you don't mind me asking, is he still alive?'

'No, he died in Frimley Park Hospital. It was only last year. It was so sad; the bowel cancer finally took him. He was on morphine at the end but he's in a much better place now; popping his clogs bless him was the best thing for him in the end.'

Just then Jayne looked at her watch.

'Look, I've got to go back to work, give me your number and I'll arrange something, perhaps you could come round for dinner. It would be nice if you could meet my husband Dave and the kids. It'll be fun,' she said.

'Are you married?'

'No, I'm supposed to be getting a divorce,' I replied.

She smiled.

'Never mind, it happens to the best of us. I lost my previous husband Mark; he died trying to save a cat from drowning in the River Wey. I've never really got over that but meeting and marrying Dave has helped a lot. He's very good with the boys and he treats them as if they're his own. I'm so proud of him,' she said.

I didn't tell her that I already knew about what happened to her first husband as I didn't want to come across as a 'know it all' but it does sound like she's had a bit of a hard life up until now. When we got back to her shop we said our goodbyes and I almost danced around the corner back to the office. It felt like I actually had a family now and although she didn't say it, going by her mannerisms I got the distinct impression that Jayne felt a bit the same.

BOOK TWO

Getting to work this morning was horrendous. The train got as far as Aldershot and then was terminated. I had to wait on the packed platform for nearly an hour for a train to Guildford and then a further thirty odd minutes for another one from there to Woking. Something had happened at Brookwood and no-one was telling us anything. No announcements, no apologies, nothing. Even the railway staff didn't seem to know what was going on. I eventually arrived at the office nearly two hours late.

Nancy had driven in from West End and was already on the telephone to someone. No-one else had managed to get in yet, not even Lisa. After about ten minutes Nancy eventually came off the phone,

'Be a darling and make me a nice coffee, lots of milk and two sugars for a change please.'

'Do you know what's up with the trains this morning?' I asked.

'I'm trying to find out; the railway people aren't answering their phones. Bloody typical! All I know is that all lines through Brookwood have been closed since around 20:45 yesterday evening. I've tried to get hold of Geoff, Ted and Lisa. Apparently they've all left home to come to work but obviously none have made it yet.'

Just then Ted appeared. Ted lives in West Byfleet these days and didn't know what was going on either.

'My train was a bit late but don't forget I'm travelling from the opposite direction to everybody else,' he said.

'Ted, would you mind getting a taxi to Brookwood and find out what the hell is going on down there?' Nancy asked.

'I can't, remember I'm covering the Sheerwater rape case and the verdict is being delivered today, I definitely need to be in court for that one,' he said.

Nancy then looked in my direction.

'Okay Jack, book yourself a taxi to Brookwood and remember to get a receipt. When you find out what's going on give me a ring. See if you can bring me back some kind of story.'

The morning was becoming even more frustrating as all the taxi companies were busy. Eventually I got hold of a guy called Eddie whose card I had found under a coffee cup on Geoff's desk.

The traffic was slow and there were tail backs in St John's right through to Brookwood Lye. I arrived at the station just before eleven o'clock, Eddie asked if I wanted him to wait for me but as his meter was still running I paid him the £4.00, got my receipt and told him to go. I hoped I might be able to get a train back. When I got to the platform a train came through in the London direction.

'First train through this morning,' someone said.

Some passengers were furious. They had been waiting hours for a train and when one did appear it didn't stop. No-one seemed to know what had happened. I saw a policeman and asked if he knew.

'Hello, I'm Jack Compton, I'm from the *Woking Tribune*, you couldn't tell me what's happened here could you?' I asked.

'Wish I could, we don't know ourselves, and in fact it looks like nothing has happened at all.'

'But why have all the lines been closed causing trains to be cancelled?'

'Our night turn boys had a call around nine o' clock last night just as they were coming on duty saying someone had been hit by a train but nothing was found, we think it's just a hoax, the BTP chaps are trying to find out more.'

'BTP?'

'Yes, British Transport Police, that's the force who should be dealing with incidents on the railway.'

After he wandered off to the station forecourt with a WPC I was left to wonder. I noticed more trains running through and something a bit more like normality being restored. A woman with a push chair asked me what had been going on. I couldn't really tell her because I didn't know apart from what the policeman had just told me. I wasn't sure that he had told me everything though. A couple of other people then joined in the conversation. One of them suggested that I went along to the porter's office.

'Ask Wilbur, he'll know,' the gentleman said.

I walked along the platform, found the office and poked my head around the door. Inside was a man of Caribbean appearance, mid-forties perhaps. He was holding a large white enamel teapot.

'Are you Wilbur?'

'I am, I am and who do I have the pleasure of meeting now?' he asked.

'I'm Jack Compton; I work for the *Woking Tribune*.'

'Well, a reporter?'

'Yes, a reporter. Do you know what happened here last night?'

'Well, when I got here this morning everything was shut down; there was a fire engine, an ambulance and about half a dozen police cars out on the forecourt. They'd been here since around nine last night. All I've done all morning is make the tea and get sworn at by my lovely passengers,' he said with a grin.

'But, do you know what actually happened?'

'All I know is that the driver of 1A69 reported hitting someone as he approached the station. Emergency services were called around twenty-one-hundred but nothing was found.'

'What's 1A69?'

'1A69 is the train ID, you know, identification number. Let me see, yes that would be the 20:35 empties from Woking to Farnham yesterday evening.'

'Empties?'

'Yes, empty rolling stock.'

I was getting confused by all the railway jargon, they seem to have their own language here and this wasn't helped by Wilbur's strong Caribbean accent.

'Where are you from, Jamaica?'

'Ha, ha man, everyone thinks that, I'm actually from Trinidad, I want to go back there when I retire, and my pension pot should be quite healthy by then.'

'How long have you worked here?'

'Since 1974, my twenty years were up last week. Another five and I get my long service award,' he said quite proudly.

'Anyway, going back to last night's incident, is there any way that I can find out what actually happened here?'

Just then I could hear a strange clanking noise. It was something coming through the fax.

'Ah this should tell us something. It's the Control Log, it's a bit late coming through this morning,' he said.

'Can I see it?'

'I'm not supposed to show you but I won't notice if you have a sly peek while I make the tea. Sugar?'

'Err, yes two please.'

The Control Log seemed to take ages coming through the fax and it looked like the machine was going to run out of ink. I guessed the bit I was waiting for was going to be at the end, so I tried to be patient and hoped that Wilbur wouldn't change his mind about letting me see it.

'There tea, I need to run along quickly and make use of the ablutions,' he said.

I noticed there was a Zerox copy machine in the corner of the office. When the last pages came through I saw the heading, 'Suspected Fatality at Brookwood'. This is it I thought. I hastily made myself a copy of the last two pages of the log before Wilbur returned. Before shoving them in my pocket I spotted a couple of references to Farnham where I live. It was then that I realised that what I call the engine sheds must be the depot where the traincrew are based. I thought that I could ask a few more questions down there on the way home later. I thanked Wilbur for his time and for the tea which tasted really awful. It was if the teabags had been used a few times already. Recycled as it's called these days.

'Do I get my name in the paper now sir?' he asked.

I laughed.

'If I can actually piece all this together and make a proper story out of it, then just maybe,' I replied.

We shook hands and I boarded the next train to Woking. It gave me a chance to read through the copy of the log item that I had procured and indeed it made for some interesting reading...

CONTROL LOG

Wednesday 13 July 1994

Private & Confidential
Not for dissemination outside the Railway Group

Item No. 73
Time of Incident: 20:45
SUSPECTED FATALITY AT BROOKWOOD

Train ID: 1A69
Units: 3417, 3402 (8 Car ECS)
Driver: FND38 Duty
Guard: FNC38 Duty

20:49

Report received from MOM of a person hit by train on DSL at Brookwood Station. Emergency services called. All lines blocked and current switched off. Incident occurred at 20:45.

21:33

Ambulance now on site.

21:43

Surrey Constabulary officers at scene awaiting BTP colleagues.

21:45

3rd Line On-Call Manager Andrew Fairbrother advised and asked for local on-call managers/supervisors to be mobilised re: care of duty for traincrew.

22:06

MOM confirms that FN38 Crew from Farnham is involved. Driver is badly shaken. Guard assisting driver in cab. Driver is Steve Callion and Guard is Bill Ashcroft.

22:08

TCS at Woking advised and will be updated of situation. Rail Supervisor Alan Perry has kindly agreed to travel using his own transport from Woking to Brookwood to assist. Med-Screen called.

22:16

Train involved is 1A69 20+39 Woking to Farnham Shed which was taken out of service at Woking due to a damaged shoe beam on 3417. No spare crew at Woking to split and run 3402 in service as 4 Car. Woking TCS confirms.

23:15

<u>MOM states that police have still not found a body</u>. Search now hampered by poor visibility due to darkness and heavy rain.

00:05 (14 JULY 1994)

Operations Director appraised of situation and requests bus replacement service for start of AM peak.

01:05

Crew taken back to Farnham via taxi. Driver has been med-screened on site.

01:35

Supervisor Perry reports from scene. "Police are beginning to have concerns about the driver's welfare. A body is yet to be found and there are no obvious signs that the train has been involved in a fatality."

04:45

Rolling stock has now been moved under caution to Farnham utilising early turn cover crew from Woking. Both units will be examined by early turn fitter when he arrives at depot. All lines to remain closed until further notice as police are now treating area as a suspected crime scene.

05:12

MOM reports from scene. Police resuming search.

06:45

MOMs changing shifts. Early turn MOM states that police have attained two eye-witness reports from passengers who were waiting for late running 2A58 Alton to Woking service on up platform.

06:55

Both reports state that a young woman in a long white pinafore style dress or gown came through side gate at the London end of Platform One, jumped and ran on to tracks into the path of 1A69 on DSL but then just seemed to vanish. This in part corroborates report given to

Supervisor Perry from Driver Callion stating that a person had been hit. Driver's report now received via fax in Control Office.

07:20

All lines remain closed. Services to London Waterloo being diverted via Guildford and Ascot from Aldershot. DEVAC clerk compiling list of delays and cancellations.

07:35

Ambulance crew stood down as nothing has been found.

07:45

Guard's report now received via fax in Control Office. Report from Guard Ashcroft states that he did not see anything as he was situated in guard's van of rear unit at time of alleged incident.

08:00

Request to open all lines for normal running declined by police.

08:02

Operations Director updated of events and is travelling by car with Woking SM Paula Thomas to observe the scene and liaise with emergency services.

08:15

NSE (SW) press officer updated regarding events.

08:35

Problems getting bus replacement services. Two single-deckers from Stagecoach Bus (Aldershot) and one from Tillingbourne obtained.

Road Transport Manager Ron Jones advises that both companies have had problems getting hold of extra drivers at short notice.

09:00

BTP advise that all lines must remain closed for at least another hour as further searches of scene are carried out.

09:45

Fitter's report received via fax from Farnham. Report states that apart from damaged shoe beam which had led to units being taken out of service at Woking, nothing else has been found. No evidence of any impact with person or animal. Report forwarded to BTP Sgt. Paul Banger at Guildford.

10:00

Lines re-opened. Delays expected until end of service due to displaced crews and rolling stock.

10:05

NSE (SW) press officer updated and advised that undertakers were not called. Incident closed.

<< END OF LOG FOR 13 JULY 1994 >>

When I got back to the office Nancy criticised me for not giving her a call as she requested. In all the furore of what was happening I had completely forgotten. I just jumped on the first available train so that I could get back as quick as I could. At least she seemed to appreciate that.

'Right, what have you been able to find out?' she asked.

'Apparently there was a suspected fatality at Brookwood just before nine o' clock last night. Police were unable to find a body and the policeman I spoke to reckons it's all a hoax.'

'Hoax? Either there's been a fatality or there hasn't!'

'That's exactly what I thought until I read this.'

I showed Nancy the pages from the Control Log that I had managed to pinch. She seemed quite impressed.

'Showing your initiative at last,' she joked.

I smiled thinking that I always show my initiative but she doesn't always see it.

'What's M.O.M?'

'I think it stands for Movements Operations Manager, I saw that on one of the other log entries as it was coming through the fax or facsimile machine as you call it.'

'It's got the train driver's name on here; perhaps we should try and interview him. Am I right in thinking that he and the guard are based at Farnham?'

'Yes, I'm planning to go into the station at Farnham on my way home later to see if I can find out anything more.'

'Good thinking but I doubt if he'll be there, he's probably off sick or even suspended going by what I'm reading here,' she said.

'I pointed out that the log item reveals that two passengers saw someone run in front of the train and then vanish.

'This is what really caught my eye.'

'Yes it's strange, quite intriguing,' she replied.

'Look, get yourself down to Farnham now. I'll call my friend Carol at the *Herald*, I'll get her to meet you there, she'll know her way round and will also know exactly who to ask about things. She's a rather large stout looking lady with short black hair and she nearly always wears a white mackintosh and green scarf, you won't miss her.'

'Is that the *Farnham Herald*?'
'What other *Herald* is there? Of course it's the *Farnham Herald*.'
Nancy laughed and then told me to be on my way.

When I got to Farnham the station was almost empty apart from a few passengers waiting for the next London train. Everywhere on the station appeared to be locked up including the ticket office. Rather than just leave I thought it was best to hang around. Just then Carol appeared but wasn't wearing a mackintosh as Nancy had described. Probably too warm for that today I thought.

'Hi, I'm Carol, you must be young Jack. Would you like to come with me?'

We walked back over the footbridge to the London bound platform and then further away from the main station building to where there was a Portakabin. She knocked on the door and then a man in a railway guard's uniform appeared.

'Oh, Hello Carol, how you doing?'

'I'm fine, thank you,' she replied.

We went inside, there were about six other railwaymen sat in there all drinking tea and reading newspapers. Some were drivers, some were guards. I think they were all getting ready to change shifts from what I could make out.

'Jack, this is Pete Finden, I've known him for years, perhaps he might be able to fill you in with what you need to know,' she said.

'Are you here about last night's suicide?' he asked.

'Suicide?'

'Yes, suicide, Steve's still very shaken by it.'

'Steve?'

'Yes, Steve Callion. Not only has he hit someone, he's been accused of making it all up, he's off sick now and his manager has arranged some counselling. I guess he won't be back to work for weeks after this.'

Just then the door opened and another man walked in.

'Is this about last night?'

'Yes,' said Pete.

Pete introduced me to the man who had just started changing out of his motorcycle leathers into a guard's uniform.

We shook hands.

'Hello, I'm Jack, Jack Compton from the *Woking Tribune*.'

'I'm Bill Ashcroft, I was the guard on that train last night and it's all a bit weird. I was in the rear guard's van when I felt Steve slam the brakes on hard. I nearly toppled out of my chair. When I got to the front cab he was shaking like a leaf. "I've hit someone, I've hit someone" he kept saying. Apart from a couple of people on the up platform there was no-one else about, so I got down and reported everything to the signalman using the SPT.'

'SPT?'

'Yes, the Signal Post Telephone. A fire engine turned up first, then a policeman and then an ambulance. Later lots more police arrived. By that time it was pissing down with rain and they started searching the line but couldn't find anything. Apparently they decided to wait until daylight this morning to carry on with the search. The MOM arranged for a taxi to take us back here to Farnham and then Tim the night duty manager debriefed us both before taking Steve home by car. I had my bike but really felt Okay, just a bit bemused by it all to be honest so I just rode home as usual.'

I told Bill that I had seen the Control Log and that it states that two witnesses had seen a woman jump under the train.

'That's interesting; we never get to see those logs. Steve will be glad to hear that, he's hoping that someone can confirm his story. I didn't see anything so I feel a bit bad that I can't help him.'

I thanked Bill and Pete for their time. Carol told me that if I played it right, I could be on to the biggest story the *Tribune* has covered for awhile.

'Look, here's my number, if you need any more help with anything, give me a call. Of course I will be writing up my own version of events for the *Herald* as the traincrew are based in Farnham but I promise I won't encroach on your take on things, I've got too many other things to do but I think you have caught a paranormal element here so good luck with that,' she said.

I got the impression that Carol was a bit anti-paranormal by the way she spoke about it. She probably doesn't believe in that sort of thing. Here though, just maybe I have the story that I've been waiting for!

2

I'm glad the weekend has finally come following all the drama on Thursday morning especially. It's been a busy week and a lot has happened. I've learned more about Tommy, probably found out all I ever will know about my father and have met a sister who until very recently didn't even know I had. I might also be on to a big story at last. It's a good time to reflect. I have thought about visiting Amanda to tell her all my news but I'm not sure how she'll react so I've decided to visit Brookwood and Knaphill again today just to have another look round and try and put things into perspective. It's an opportunity to try and kill two birds with one stone to see if I could put some sense into the incident and to see if I could find out more about Tommy.

I decided to go back into The Crown pub in Knaphill. There was a different woman behind the bar and she was much younger, prettier and friendlier than the one who was there before. She was stroking a big tabby cat that was lying on the bar. In the corner there were two men chatting and playing dominoes. One of them was Philip Janner, the man I went to see the last time I was over here.

'Hello, remember me, I'm Jack, we spoke the other week,' I said.

'Oh yes, how did you get on with Hope Pengelley, did you find out anymore?'

'Yes, she actually remembered my grandfather, he was good friends with her late husband apparently,' I replied.

'That's good news, now talking of news; you're a reporter aren't you. What happened at Brookwood Station the other night?'

I told him all I knew and said that it was all a bit of a mystery and that the police think it's just a hoax and that there may be something a bit wrong with the train driver. I also told him that I'd seen the official railway control log and about the two witnesses who say they saw a woman jump in front of the train and then simply disappear.

'That's very interesting; something very similar happened there a few years ago back in 1982 I think. It may have even been on the corresponding date. Police looked around for a body then but nothing was found.'

'Has there ever been a real fatality at Brookwood before?' I asked.

'Oh quite a few over the years, there's also a story of a headless ghost in Foxhills Tunnel.'

'Foxhills Tunnel?'

'Yes, the tunnel between Brookwood and Ash Vale, a young lad was killed there in the late 1960s; it's thought that the ghost is him.'

'What was the date on Wednesday?' he asked.

'13th July.'

'I'll have to look that one up, I've got a chronological record back home somewhere detailing all local railway incidents and events going right back to the days of the London & South Western Railway as it was known. My father left it for me, he was mad keen on the old steam trains and used to be the station master at Woking before the war,' he said.

I asked him if he could tell me more about the asylum and what it was like.

'I could tell you lots of things about the place, a good number of people who live in Knaphill used to work there and have their own stories, some are quite harrowing and absolutely beyond belief. It's hard to believe that so many bad things went on over there. In some ways it's good that parts of the place are being pulled down but there are already stories of ghosts and strange happenings even in the new buildings which have only just gone up,' he said.

I noticed that his friend was becoming quite impatient and wanted to carry on with their game of dominoes.

'Thanks Philip,' I said.

'Call me Phil, I hate being called Philip. My mother always used to call me Philip when she was telling me off as a boy,' he joked.

'Can I contact you again at some point, I'm trying to put a story together about the station incident and it would be great if I could get a historical connection somehow.'

'I've got your number, I'll give you a ring if I find anything,' he said.

I thanked him for his time and nodded at his friend before saying goodbye to the barmaid who was still making a fuss of the cat.

Outside it was quite warm although the sun was very hazy. I was still feeling quite thirsty so I decided to walk back down towards the station and stop off at a pub called the Nags Head. The place was a bit run down but I remember Tommy had mentioned it a couple of times in one or two of his diaries. An old man who was sitting in the corner by the piano told me that the pub was often frequented by navvies who worked on the Basingstoke Canal in the late 1700s and then by railway workers some fifty years later. He seemed to know quite a lot about local history and asked me if I knew Phil Janner.

'Yes, I've just been speaking to him up the road in The Crown.'

'He's a bag full of local knowledge, he can normally pull things out of a hat in a split second when it comes to that kind of stuff,' he said.

I seemed to remember someone telling me something similar before. All worth bearing in mind for future reference I thought.

When I got back to the station Wilbur the porter was there tending to some plants in a big wooden tub on the platform.

'Hello, remember me, I'm Jack from the *Woking Tribune*, we met the other morning,' I said.

'Yeah man, I remember you, you got my name in that paper of yours yet?'

'I'm still working on the story, today is technically my day off, I don't usually work weekends,' I told him.

'Lucky you, one day off in fourteen is all I get and that's usually every other Sunday,' he said with a laugh.

I then noticed that my train was about to arrive on the opposite platform.

'Just one thing sir,' he said.

'What?'

'There was a passenger here earlier who said that he saw a woman go under that train the other night. He's gone up to London today, not sure when he's coming back but he gave me his name and number, take it quick, now run,' he said.

I thanked Wilbur and got to the other platform with just seconds to spare. The guard gave me a dirty look because I'd jumped on just as the train was about to move but fortunately he didn't say anything. I looked at the piece of paper Wilbur had just given me. It was someone called Reginald Smythe. The name seems quite familiar but I'm not sure why.

Back home I decided to look through Tommy's diaries again. The name was bugging me. I've seen it written down somewhere quite recently and I'm sure that there's a connection somewhere with my grandfather, perhaps at the asylum. In the 1929 diary there are a lot of references to a Reginald but at first I couldn't find a surname. I kept flicking back and then there it was: an entry about Reginald Smythe on 20th October 1929. Tommy describes him as the 'quiet man'. There are a few more entries relating to his apparent disappearance and then on 24th November it states that a body is found. Reginald's body had been discovered upside down in a deep well in the asylum grounds. Weighed down by stones with a mask over his face in an apparent suicide it seems. I shudder now. Is this all just a strange coincidence, or is something else going on?

3

It has been very difficult trying to get to sleep over the weekend. On Saturday evening I stayed up drinking until about three in the morning. Two bottles of red wine polished off and Sunday was similar. I've decided not to tell anyone about my thoughts, how the event at Brookwood Station could be connected to something Tommy had written down in one of his diaries all those years ago. I'm sure it must be just a co-incidence but the whole scenario has got an air of creepiness about it and now I'm worried that people might think that I'm delusional. I need to do a bit more digging and find out a lot more but I must keep my thoughts 'Personal!' If anything out of the ordinary has happened then I'm sure I will find out but the whole thing is starting to consume me and just at a time when it felt like I was getting my life back on track. I need to be strong and focused; I must not let things get the better of me this time.

In the office Geoff has been caught smoking and Nancy has just given him a bollocking even though I know that she smokes secretly in her office when it's quiet. The strong smell of Rothman's gives her away. Eventually they both emerge and Geoff returns rather sheepishly to his desk. Nancy came over and asked me if I had managed to find out any more about the incident at Brookwood. I told her that I had met one of the traincrew, the guard but he didn't know much because of where he was situated in the train at the moment the alleged fatality took place.

'Alleged, I always like that word, it's a good get out clause for a lot of things,' she said.

I told her that Carol from the *Farnham Herald* was very helpful and was able to find someone who knew the guard.

'Yes, she's good with things like that but we do reciprocate, we do the same for her sometimes, especially when Ted needs a hand with one of his court cases. A little earlier I was speaking to a Sergeant Banger from the British Transport Police. They are closing the file on the incident and have recommended that the train driver is offered some kind of medical help, that's if he's not disciplined.'

'I know, he's been offered counselling already,' I told her.

'What about these so-called witnesses?' she asked.

'Yes, I think I need to see if I can get something from the witnesses to add some credibility to the story. Perhaps they can shed some more light on the whole thing,' I said.

I hesitated but decided not to say anything about the contact details Wilbur the porter had given me mainly because of the connection I had made with what I found in one of Tommy's diaries.

'I did ask Sergeant Banger if I could have sight of their statements but they're confidential. The driver, what's his name, Steve Callion could be prosecuted for wasting police time,' she said.

'That's a bit harsh. Do you think it could actually come to that?'

'Oh yes, I've seen people charged with that kind of thing before.'

I wondered.

'Look, something very strange has happened here. Do you know Esther who does our Horoscope column?'

'Obviously I've heard of her but have never had the pleasure of meeting her.'

'Her horoscopes are published in all the local newspapers belonging to our group, She lives on the Isle of Wight, she's also a psychic medium, I know her pretty well, I'll see if she'd be interested in coming up to Woking for a day or two. This kind of thing is right up her street.'

Esther Whitehawk is quite famous. I think I've seen her on the telly a couple of times and she was the editor of *Spirit Union* magazine. I asked Nancy if that was her.

'Yes, she made her name on one of the breakfast television programmes but Satellite TV is beginning to take over now, the magazine she worked for went under and she's ended up on the sidelines and in obscurity for some reason. I think that's why she writes the column for us now.'

I've never been interested in horoscopes; they annoy me a bit, what's said never seems to happen to me anyway so I always try to avoid them.

'There's another person who could help us.'
'Who?'
'The Reverend.'
'Reverend?'

'Yes the Reverend, the Reverend Nathaniel Bream.'
'Never heard of him,' I said.
'He's one of the main contributors to the *Fortean Times*, I was at university with him and it's time for me to call in a favour or two. He's actually a scientist who specialises in the science of paranormal activity and carries out in-depth research on strange phenomena and prodigies. He's a bit of a sceptic as far as the spiritual world is concerned but it should be good to have him around. It will help maintain a balanced view on things.'
'*Fortean Times*?'
'Yes, it's a specialist magazine that deals with the unexplained and supernatural. Don't worry, he's the one person who could assist in getting to the bottom of this and help us build a real story or feature. It has to be done,' she said.

Now I worry that my story is going to be taken over by other people and that they will get all the credit instead of me. I told Nancy what I was thinking.

'No don't worry; this sort of thing has been done before. We all collaborate to get to the facts and then write our own version of events. We share the information and eventually it helps push up the sales figures. Remember that we could do with a story like this to boost circulation. I promise, it will be your name at the top of the article,' she said.

'So what happens next?'

'We need to get a meeting arranged with The Reverend, Esther and ourselves to see if we can find a rational explanation for everything that happened down there the other night.'

'I know a local historian, his name is Phil Janner. Could I ask him to come along?' I asked.

'I've heard of him, yes all the more the merrier, he could help us sew some of the facts together if necessary and it's always useful having someone like Phil around when it comes to these kind of things,' she said.

'Right, I'll phone the others and see if we can set a date, I'll be looking for Wednesday or very early Thursday morning. If we can get a story into this week's edition even if it's just a few lines that would be great, we can then run a special feature when we have more substance behind what really happened.'

Now the pressure is on. I don't actually have a telephone number for Phil Janner but I phoned The Crown pub in Knaphill and left a message there for him to phone me. I hope that works.

I've just noticed Lisa hasn't been at work today. I knocked on Nancy's door.

'Hello, I've just noticed, I haven't seen Lisa today, is she alright?'

'Yes, she's away until the end of next week on a course.'

'Course?'

'Yes, course, I've given her Clarissa's job and I've managed to fit her in on a junior reporter's seminar at short notice. She'll be back in the office next Friday. Beryl is going to help me out with all the secretarial stuff until I can find someone else,' she said.

In a way I'm glad Lisa has got the job. Perhaps her devious side has worked for her after all. It will be interesting to see what happens with her next I thought.

I managed to get a brief article together for this week's deadline based on what I know so far. People will at least want to know why all the trains were delayed I thought...

Unexplained Incident Halts Trains at Brookwood Station

Police are still investigating an incident at Brookwood Railway Station amid fears that a person had been hit by a train on the evening of Wednesday 13th July.

The incident occurred at around 8:45pm causing severe disruption to services as trains were delayed, diverted and cancelled right through to the end of service and up until Thursday lunch-time.

British Transport Police confirmed that emergency services were called to the scene just before 9pm after receiving a report that someone, believed to be a young woman had been struck by a train. Officers failed to locate a body and were preparing a report for British Rail as the *Tribune* went to press.

It is alleged that the driver of the train who cannot be named for legal reasons may have suffered a 'medical episode' on his approach to the station and a full investigation is under way. Police are appealing for witnesses and are asking for anyone with information to come forward.

4

I've just been introduced to Esther Whitehawk. I can honestly say that she's one of the scariest looking women I have ever met but at the same time I find her quite interesting. She is definitely an advocate of what she believes in and is very enthusiastic. She has long straight black hair, pronounced arched eyebrows and piercing grey eyes with lots of carefully applied make-up. Probably what you would expect a psychic medium to look like in fact. I noticed that she kept looking at me quite strangely but I didn't think too much of it. Shortly afterwards the Reverend Bream walked into the office and Nancy introduced him to me and Esther. His handshake was very limp.

'Right Jack, you're in charge from now on, I have a series of meetings with Mr Hackett over the next few days and I want to make sure that I still have a job and can keep my holiday plans intact so please go and get me a good story, make it your own feature and don't forget to give me a ring if you need anything,' she said.

I took Esther and the Reverend around the corner to the station and we caught the 11:25am train to Brookwood. I couldn't help notice that Esther was again looking at me quite strangely as we sat in the carriage, it was almost as if she was looking over my right shoulder all the time but I didn't want to say anything in case there was something wrong with her eyes. When the train arrived at Brookwood Phil Janner was there and he suggested that we went through the underpass and on to the other platform to Wilbur's office.

'He's making the tea for us,' he said.

'Oh God,' I thought and warned the others of my last experience drinking a cup of Wilbur's tea. They laughed. When we reached his office the teas were already poured and he'd left some digestive biscuits out for us.

'I'll leave you fine people here, I have some hanging baskets to attend to,' he said.

Just before he left the room I took him to one side and asked him to describe Reginald Smythe, the man who had said that he had seen the incident and had left his contact details.

'I don't remember him that well, it's all a bit vague now, he was there in front of me one minute and then was gone the next, he went up on the next train to London I think, although I'm not one-hundred per cent sure.'

This seemed to slightly contradict some of what he'd told me before.

'But can you actually tell me what he looked like?' I asked.

'Average, just average but I do remember that he spoke quite funny. Short sharp sentences, almost as if he didn't really want to speak at all,' he said.

I wondered.

I then introduced Phil Janner to everyone. He had turned up with a small brown attaché case full of old papers and files.

'Some of these go right back to 1850, they're all recorded incidents on this stretch of railway line, I also have some old newspaper cuttings going back to the start of the century. These could also be useful,' he said.

Phil then suggested that someone should chair the meeting and asked if anyone had come up with an agenda.

'No, sorry, I'm just here to report on what may or may not have happened. Esther Whitehawk and the Reverend Bream are here because they have their own interest in what may have occurred but I'm hoping they can assist me with my story as well,' I said.

'Okay. Look, I've chaired meetings before, let's give this some kind of structure and see where it leads us too,' he said.

We all agreed.

I had to be careful not to let it slip that I had secretly copied the railway Control Log item about the incident. I also didn't want to mention that I had my own theory about Reginald Smythe. I was still worried that there might be a connection with what I had read in one of Tommy's diaries.

'Let's go out on the platform again and get a feel of the place,' Esther suggested.

I think that comment was just an excuse to get away from Wilbur's tea! On the platform she started looking at me again and this time stroked the side of my face, it was all very weird. She just smiled but still didn't say anything. I then noticed that the Reverend was frantically scribbling notes down into a small green WH Smith notebook. He doesn't look like a very religious person; he was just wearing an old Wishbone Ash T shirt, jeans and white Dunlop Green Flash training shoes. I noticed Phil had brought out a particular journal dated 1931; he was excitedly thumbing through the pages.

'What was the date the other Wednesday?' he asked.

'13th July.'

'Oh yes, I remember you telling me now.'

'Why?'

'In 1931 on the same date there was a fatality here, it looks like it may have occurred at exactly the same time of the evening. What time did the incident happen?' He asked.

'Just before 9pm according to what I've found out so far,' I said.

'Do you know the precise time?'

'Well, it's just that 20:49 is when the incident was officially recorded but I do know that the train left Woking at 20:39,' I said without revealing my source of information.

'Ten or eleven minutes to get from Woking to Brookwood?'

'It normally only takes six minutes but the train had been taken out of service at Woking because of a defect and was running as empty rolling stock to the depot at Farnham, the incident must have occurred at around 20:45 which would have given another four minutes for it to reported,' I said quite confidently.

By now Wilbur had returned to the group and agreed with my calculation.

'The stock was running in a Q Path and the Q path is timed to leave Woking at 20:39 whenever it's required.'

'Q Path?'

'Yes Q Path. It's a slot in the timetable where a train can go from A to B if it needs to be taken out of service. Q Paths are also used for freight trains and special services like charter trains, Royal Ascot week is an example,' he added.

I think I knew what he was trying to say but was quite flummoxed by it all. Again the railway jargon and Wilbur's strong accent were getting the better of me.

Just then Phil butted in rather abruptly.

'Yes there is a record here of a fatality on the 13th July 1931 involving a train from Waterloo that was running as a special charter to Southampton Docks to connect with a cruise liner bound for New York. The train was delayed for over two hours but that's all it says,' he remarked.

'This is all very interesting,' said Esther.

The Reverend nodded in agreement. I hadn't really heard him speak yet which I found quite odd although I did get the impression that he was listening very hard to everything that was being said. I think he was actually writing his story up as we went along. Just then Esther asked me to walk with her to the London end of Platform One. A train had just departed so the station was empty.

'There's a young lady standing with you, twenties, dark red hair, ringlets, she has amazing green eyes, do you know anyone who has passed over recently?' she asked.

I shuddered and felt goose-bumps up and down my arms.

'No, the only bereavement I've ever experienced was when my mother died when I was about four. Anyway she was dark haired and had brown eyes.'

'This young lady is holding up the letter 'T'. Would that be significant to you in anyway?' she asked.

I was just about to say 'No' and then I thought of Tommy.

'Well actually...' and then I paused.

'Well?'

'I'm not sure, perhaps I'm imagining too much,' I said.

Just then Phil Janner walked over and interrupted again and suggested that we could find out more.

'Look, if we go through the old death registers dating back to the 13th July 1931 we should be able to find a name. I think I know where to look,' he said.

'But we have no description of the person who was killed back then,' I said.

'Yes we have, she's been standing beside you and I've just told you what she looks like. If we come up with a young lady aged around mid-twenties then I think we will have found our spirit,' Esther answered.

'Spirit?'

'Yes, spirit.'

'I think who ever that poor train driver saw jump in front of him is actually the spirit of the person who died here in 1931. Did someone say that she was wearing a white gown or pinafore style dress?'

'Yes, it's in the Control Log item that I read. Apparently she came through that side gate, ran across the tracks, jumped in front of the train and just vanished.'

Just then the Reverend spoke up.

'I've heard of this sort of thing before. It's a kind of apparition repetition. It's where a ghost for want of a better word relives the anniversary of their actual death. Those susceptible to spirit will see it while most of us don't,' he said.

'Apparition?'

'Yes, many people think that an apparition can be a private revelation as it were: a personal message received and communicated in a personal way and this may explain why Esther has been showing a special interest in you, apparently it's quite a phenomenon although I still have my own reasons for doubting the very existence of a presence and this is where my own views differ quite a bit from those of Esther's,' he said.

I felt quite shocked by what he said. I really need to let all this sink in before I say anything to anyone I thought.

An excited Phil got more and more involved with the conversation.

'That explains why there may have been a couple of similar incidents like this here before. Look, a train doesn't always run in this time slot. Like Wilbur said, it's a Q Path. It's only when a train does run that there's a possible incident,' he said.

'How can you describe them as incidents, if there is no evidence of a body,' I asked.

'Trust me, if it affects the train service whether anything has actually happened or not, it's still an incident,' Phil explained.

Esther nodded and agreed.

'Yes, believe it or not these incidents are quite common. If we could do more to find out this young lady's name then maybe I can help her and put her poor soul to rest,' she said.

'Can you actually do that, it all seems a bit far-fetched to me?'

'I'm very sure, if I'm wrong then I will be putting over twenty years of credibility at risk and I'm certainly not going to do that now.'

Just then the Reverend interrupted. 'Although I have my own alternative views, Esther is probably the very best at what she does. She's helped many famous people contact their loved ones who have passed over, she has a great reputation for giving people closure over their bereavement issues,' he said.

It's been a long day and I think the Reverend now has enough information on the incident to submit a story to his magazine. Just before he left he gave me a couple of tips on how to write my feature article for the *Tribune* which I found very useful. Phil Janner is going to London tomorrow to try and get a name from the Public Records Office and I have decided to plough through all the archives I can to see if I can get a cross-match of the incident. Esther is still about for another day or two and has asked to meet me again. By the end of tomorrow I hope to have my first big feature ready to give to Nancy but there are so many unanswered questions and I'm still wondering about what the Reverend said about apparitions and personal messages. I also wonder about the man Wilbur had spoken to who calls himself Reginald Smythe.

It wasn't until I got home that something obvious began to hit me in the face. It was then that I remembered my conversation with Mrs Pengelley up in Knaphill on the first Saturday I went over. I got Tommy's diaries back out and began sifting through the pages. 13th July 1931, something just has to be here I thought. When I found the date there was no entry relating to any particular incident. I decided to read on through the next couple of pages and then I found it...

15th July 1931

"There was about a minute's silence where I just kept looking at the ground and then he told me.
'She got out on Monday night. The window was left open in the ablutions and she slid down the diagonal rainwater pipe and made good her escape. We wouldn't have known but there was an accident down at the railway station involving the 20:05 hours Waterloo to Southampton Docks. Someone had been hit and smashed to pieces. The constabulary contacted the Medical Superintendent when they found a note on the body linking it to the asylum. We were all called down there immediately to assist the railwaymen. The driver of the engine was in a right old state and the passengers were getting annoyed with us because they had a boat to catch to the Americas. The incident made them late. I didn't care for them toffs, if they missed their boat, I'm glad.' He said.
I still couldn't say anything. It was a lot to take in."

I think Tommy was referring to what he had been told by one of the wardens. I had seen the entry before but hadn't read it in full mainly because of his poor handwriting. It looks like it took two days before he was made aware of the incident. Other entries refer to the name Maisie, the very name Mrs Pengelley mentioned. Now I am left to wonder! What if the incidents are connected? What if Esther Whitehawk is actually right about the presence of a spirit and is telling the truth? What if apparitions do have personal connections? I have to ask myself these questions. I need to understand what the hell is going on but most of all I need to compose myself and make sure that it's not just my imagination getting the better of me.

5

I didn't sleep a wink last night; I just lay there awake and watched the shadows racing across the ceiling as it began to get light. I couldn't wait to get into the office this morning and find out more about what was going on. I mustn't reveal what I now think is definitely a personal connection. I need to carry on as normal, like nothing has happened. I need to get to grips with myself; after all I still had a story to write up.

In the office Beryl was sitting at Lisa's desk typing up some notes that Geoff had given her.

'Be a love and make the coffee, I'm a bit snowed under,' she whispered.

I gathered up the cups and went into the kitchen area, just then Esther walked in.

'Good morning Jack, how are you today?'

'I'm fine thanks.'

'Are you sure?'

'Yes why?'

'That young lady is still with you, I can see her in my mind's eye hanging off your shoulder,' she said.

'What young lady?'

'You know which young lady.'

'I don't,' I said but felt guilty about lying.

'Tommy, who's Tommy? She keeps calling out for Tommy?'

This time the goose bumps on my arms were even more evident and Esther noticed.

'I've hit a raw nerve, haven't I?' she said. 'I'm never wrong about these things!'

Just then I heard Geoff calling my name...

'Where's Jack? Jack! Phone call, someone called Phil Janner.'

I looked at the clock and noticed that most of the morning had gone already. I was happy to go to the phone as it took me away from the conversation I was having with Esther but I could sense her hovering behind me in the corner.

'Good Morning Phil.'

'I've got a couple of names here, both died in Brookwood on the same day. 13th July 1931.'

'What names?'

'Emma Lamplugh aged 78 and Maisie Albright, 26. Emma Lamplugh was a spinster who lived in Connaught Road and Maisie Albright who was an artist. It shows her last known address as 1, Broadway, Knaphill, the asylum's postal address dating back to around that time. Does either of these two names ring a bell? My guess it's the younger one,' he said.

'Yes, that would be my guess too,' I replied.

When I put the phone down Esther pulled up a chair beside me.

'Look, you can talk to me about this privately if you prefer, let me take you to lunch somewhere quiet, I can see that you have some heavy burdens on your shoulders, I'll square things with Nancy for you so we can grab a bit more time and have a proper break.'

'But I have a story to write up, I was going to start that after I had finished making the coffees, I have a deadline to meet.'

'Like I said, I will speak with Nancy and when we come back after lunch I will help you with the story. I must be on the 16:55 to Portsmouth though. It's the last train which connects with my ferry otherwise I'll have a long wait later.' She said.

I agreed and decided to start on my article anyway but thought it best to make sure that I left out any personal references and just stick to the known facts of the incident. I knew it was going to be hard and I was worried that my first big piece for the paper was going to be ruined by everything that I was beginning to find out. Just then Esther walked back over to my desk...

'Right, lunchtime, Jack, now, Nancy has recommended a little bistro bar around the corner, Enzo's, do you know it?'

'Yes, my sister works quite close to it; I only walked past it the other day.'

'Have you ever been in there before?'

'No, never.'

When we arrived Esther said something to the waiter and we went to a seating area upstairs, don't worry, we won't be disturbed up here, the waiter said that he would keep everyone else downstairs for awhile, I told him that we're from the *Tribune* and I gave him a little something,' she said.

I smiled but felt quite nervous.'

'Look, the best thing I can do is give you a personal reading, if it connects with the story we're covering then so be it but please trust me, I will help you to keep everything separate.'

I actually began to feel more relaxed in her company although her piercing grey eyes still unnerved me despite her reassurances.

'She's still with me, isn't she?' I said.

'Who Maisie? Yes she is, she won't let go, she's trying to connect with you and she wants you to know everything about Tommy. Who is Tommy?'

'He was my grandfather.'

'Then that explains it, 1931, how old would he have been then?'

'Err about twenty-five or twenty-six,' I said.

'How would they have known each other?'

'They were both patients at the lunatic asylum down the road.'

'Brookwood?'

'Yes, that's it.'

'Is that the one that's just closed down?'

'Mostly, there are still bits of it left while they still wait to re-house some of the patients. "Care in the Community" I think it's called.'

'That's remarkable; did you know that mental patients are more prone to connect with spirit than anyone else?'

'I've heard that before but in the end my grandfather proved that he wasn't a lunatic and I'm sure from what I've read in some of his diaries, this Maisie lady and many others weren't either,' I replied.

'That's astonishing, tell me more about your grandfather, you know, just snapshots and things like that...'

'I don't want to say too much but I began to find out more about him whilst I was seeking information about my father who died just before I was born. I have an aunt who lives in Camberley, she gave me lots of stuff including his old RAF flight jacket, books and diaries and other things. All I really know for sure is that he was born in 1904 or 1905, was sent to the Brookwood Lunatic Asylum in 1929, absconded from there a couple of years later, joined the army and then somehow ended up in the RAF. He died four years ago,' I said.

'That's quite a comprehensive summary.'

'To be honest that's all I want to say, I'm feeling quite uncomfortable about all this now,' I replied.

'You need to be able to breathe, take deep breaths, I'm trying to help you understand that there are good people in spirit who are looking over you, including Maisie but she's a lost soul and she needs to be properly laid to rest. Her spirit needs to be freed from the turmoil that she finds herself in.'

'Why does she need to tell me about Tommy?'

'It's possibly her way of putting herself to rest. She thinks that he has blamed himself all his life for what happened to her. She wants you to know that it wasn't his fault. I think that the incident at Brookwood railway station is her final cry for help; you know the repetitive apparition thing that we were talking about. It's also possible that she thinks you're Tommy, you're about the same age as she is in spirit.'

'But if she's in Spirit as you call it then she would have met Tommy, by now wouldn't she?'

'Not necessarily. Not if he's on another plain. Remember, there was a big time lapse between the dates when they passed over. It's possible she just hasn't found him yet!'

'How do you know all this?'

'I just know, it's called uniting the spirit, it's a gift, some of us have it but many people don't. Some psychic mediums even have a spiritual guide to help them connect with those who have passed to the other side. I prefer to make that connection myself, speak directly to the person I'm looking for but I do have a guide if I need her.'

'Well if you don't mind me saying, it's all gobbledygook to me, I don't believe any of it, well at least I'm trying not to.'

'There you are, you do believe, you just admitted it by saying what you did.'

'Okay, Okay look, I've had a few psychological problems recently and the last thing I need now is for everything to get out of hand. I don't want people thinking that I'm some kind of nutter all over again. I'm just about getting my life sorted out and I don't want all this excitement to spoil it.'

'So sorry, I didn't realise.'

'Don't worry; I'm probably just being over sensitive.'

'Can I make a suggestion?'

'What?'

'Let me finish my work here, let's see where it leads and then you can feel free to judge me afterwards.'

'That sounds fair but I need to keep all of this personal stuff out of my article and that's going to be very difficult if I don't want to give the game away,' I said.

'Go and write your follow-up story, be professional then I can discreetly edit it for you if you like before you submit it to Nancy, will you trust me?'

'Yes, I suppose, well of course, thank you!'

Esther smiled. We looked at the time and made our way back to the office.

'Get that story done by four o'clock at the latest, that will give me time to run my red pen through it,' she said.

'You sound like an editor,' I joked.

'I was once and that was a long time ago but that's another story,' she laughed.

I wondered and then remembered that she used to edit a spiritual magazine.

Back in the office I eventually got the nucleus of the article done. Esther seemed to take an age going through it and I noticed that she was busy changing things around with her pen. When she passed it back there were lots of things crossed out and a couple of things added.

'There, it's still your article, I've taken out the padding, all you have now is the pure facts and that's all the reader will want to know. I'm sure Nancy will accept it Okay, but beware, other things may develop yet and you may be able to give it more substance. It's not time-sensitive so don't rush too much but don't leave it too long either, readers will want to know more quite quickly,' she said.

I thanked her for an interesting couple of days but I was still not really sure about everything. I normally keep an open mind about these things but it does seem that she asked a lot of questions before saying anything herself so it's hard not to be sceptical.

I made a copy of the article before placing the original in Nancy's tray; unfortunately too late for this week's print deadline so I wondered what she'll say about it in the morning.

On the way home I decided to stop off for a pint at my local The Lamb pub in Abbey Street. It's a nice quiet place in the early evenings where you can sit and think. I've been going back through some of the things that Esther has been telling me over the last two days. Wondering if there's any credibility or truth in what she's said. She managed to tell me quite a lot in the time that I was with her and especially when we were walking back from Enzo's around to the office. She explained that a psychic medium works as an intermediary between the living and the world of spirit and that she can listen to and relay messages from those on the other side. She also told me that a spirit can control a medium's body and speak through it by using it as a channel for communication. There are two main categories of mediumship, both the 'mental' and the 'physical'. Esther claims that she can simply 'tune in' to the spirit world by listening, sensing or even seeing spirits through her mind's eye. This is how she was able to see Maisie holding up the letter 'T' she told me.

'If you persevere long enough you will get the answer that you're looking for but sometimes you have to be very patient,' she said.

One thing I don't understand is that if Tommy and Maisie are both dead, why haven't they been able to connect with one another in the spirit world? I know Esther mentioned something about different plains due to the time lapse between their deaths but all of that has confused me even more and I'm still wondering about Reginald Smythe. Did Wilbur actually speak to a ghost? All this intrigues me, scares me and yet in a funny way it's now hard to actually disbelieve.

6

Lisa was back in the office this morning with a spring in her step and full of all the mumbo-jumbo from her course in London.

'Make the coffee...' Geoff demanded almost sarcastically.

'No chance, I'm one of you now,' Lisa retorted.

Geoff's face was a picture as he stood up and made his way to the kitchen area. Just then Nancy appeared with Beryl.

'Don't worry we have a new office junior joining us tomorrow, he's on his induction today,' said Nancy.

'He?' asked Ted looking rather surprised. 'That's a girl's job!'

'Not anymore, we're equal opportunity employers now, if a man applies and he's suitable we have to take him on.'

'He must be queer then if he wants a woman's job,' said Geoff as he reappeared with his hastily made cup of coffee.

'Actually he is, I mean, no, I mean, he's gay, you know what I mean,' said Nancy in a bit of a fluster.

'Yes, get it right!' snapped Geoff. His expression became one of thunder and then suddenly morphed into a smile.

Lisa, Ted and Beryl were all laughing in the background just as Mr Hackett and another man walked in through the side door.

'Good morning all, nice to see that you're all enjoying yourselves. I hope that you're all finding some good stories to print,' he said with a frown.

Nancy went over to him and apologised for all the frivolity.

'Don't worry, if I've got a happy ship then there is a better chance of getting results and pushing up circulation figures,' he said.

'So who is this gentleman?' Nancy asked rather nervously.

'Yes sorry, this is Duncan Sanchez from Deloitte's.'

'Deloitte's?'

'Yes, they are our appointed auditors. Duncan will be here today and tomorrow and will be looking at our filing systems, how we've been transferring archived data from the fiche to the computers, how we operate our hardware and software and also time and motion.'

'Time and motion what's that?' Beryl asked.

Nancy butted in, 'the time it takes to carry out certain tasks,' she said.

'How long it takes to go for a piss and shit more like,' quipped Geoff.

Ted laughed and I tried not to snigger. All the women looked embarrassed and Nancy looked at Geoff with such a glare she could have killed him stone dead.

'Right, your office Ms Salem,' said Mr Hackett.

Eventually the auditor came out and Beryl made him a cup of tea. He started asking all of us some awkward questions, where we lived, our commuting times, when we took our breaks, who smoked and those sorts of things. I could see that Geoff was trying to avoid him but eventually Mr Sanchez had him cornered.

'How long have you worked here?' he asked.

'Oh, I would say about fifteen years or so now.'

'Do you enjoy your work?'

'When I'm left alone to get on with it.'

'Do you feel that you can be trusted?'

'What sort of question is that? Who the bloody hell have you been talking to about me?' he said angrily.

'No-one, it's just my job to ask, look, these are standard questions, nothing personal here, I promise.'

'Ah, that's alright then,' said Geoff in retreat.

I noticed that Lisa was sat within earshot writing a lot of things down. Despite her grand entrance this morning she's been very quiet, particularly since Mr Hackett arrived in the office. Maybe she's trying to give him a good impression I thought. The auditor eventually left around 4:15pm and Geoff made his excuses and also left. Ted was in court and Beryl had gone out to get some sundries for Nancy. I noticed Lisa looking over in my direction so felt compelled to ask how her course had gone.

'Very well, it was very intense and there was one hell of a lot to learn,' she said.

'So what next, has Nancy given you any specific areas to cover yet?'

'Not really but she's asked me to shadow Ted until further notice, he's decided to retire a little earlier than anticipated and that will be just before Christmas. Nancy wants me to be up to speed with everything by then,' she said.

'But Ted's the senior reporter?'

'I know but Nancy wants me to take over his role as there are no other suitable applicants,' she said.

'Excuse me, but his job hasn't even been advertised yet and what about me and Geoff? We should have a chance to apply before anyone else!'

'It's not quite like that, said Lisa just as Mr Hackett appeared.

'Come on, get your things, I've got a little treat lined up for you,' he said to Lisa as her face lit up.

Nancy was standing in her doorway and just winked at me from behind his back. After they left I asked her what was going on.

'They're going out together, apparently he visited the hotel where Lisa was staying on her course last week and they've been inseparable ever since,' she said.

'So that's how you get the top jobs in journalism, you sleep with the boss!' I said rather foolishly.

'Well it hasn't worked for me and it certainly hasn't worked for you, has it?' Nancy joked.

'Anyway, how's this Brookwood story going, have you found out any more information for me yet?'

'The completed article is still in your in tray where I left it,' I said.

'Well then let's go through it together. I definitely want it in the next issue if it's good enough.'

She spent a good twenty minutes thumbing through, carefully examining each paragraph. In fact I think she must have gone through it two or three times and then she eventually looked at me over the top of her glasses.

'Flawless, absolutely flawless, I will put a leader on the front page and we'll include a feature inside but I still want a bit more. Readers will want to know what's behind all this and there's nothing like a bit of the supernatural to get the grey matter working.'

I was a bit disappointed; I thought she would have put it in the paper straight away.

After work I caught the No.34 bus to Camberley and walked down to Watchetts Road. It's been a few weeks since I last saw Amanda and I noticed that she's looking quite frail and gaunt. Too many cigarettes and too much alcohol and I don't think that she's eating very much. It was quite cold for a summer's evening so she was wrapped up warm in a thick green cardigan but she still shivered as she gave me a big hug and told me how warm I was. I think she knows that she's been struggling but she just won't acknowledge her current poor state of health or concede that there's anything wrong.

'Have you got any further looking up our Tommy?' she asked.

'Yes, quite a lot really,' I replied.

It was then that I realised that I shouldn't really say too much more as it I could let it slip that I've found out more about my father.

'You seem quite evasive,' she said.

'Sorry but I need to be honest. I'm not really sure how to tell you but I've found out quite a lot and I don't want to hurt you by what I'm about to tell you.'

'You won't, shall I tell you what I know about what you know?' She said rather cryptically.

'If you like...'

'I know that you've found out all about your father, well nearly all. I also know that you've met with your sister Jayne and I know that you've met a lady who knew your grandfather from his days at the asylum in Knaphill or Brookwood as it's known.'

'How?'

'I just know,' she said looking at me rather strangely.

I sensed that any barriers may at last be coming down.

'Ok, please tell me more about my father, Lionel.'

'I don't need to. My old friend Mary Hutton or Mary Turner as she's known these days, you know the woman who you spoke to in the Four Horse Shoes the other week has been to see me. She told me about your conversation. She thinks you are a very pleasant boy. A strapping lad as she put it.'

I smiled.

'Why has there been all this secrecy though?'

'It's all about the other Jack, Big Jack. He really was the cuckold in all of this and your father was the instigator. Both your mother and

Laura Dombrowski or O'Leary as she eventually became, your half-sister's mother loved him very much but they loved your father too; or at least said they did! Your father was quite a slim man, very fit and handsome whilst Big Jack was quite the opposite. They were all hippies and were always swapping and changing, exchanging their partners, a four way tryst as some people called it. Your mother even had a lesbian fling with Laura and at one stage it all got very confusing and out of hand. Sometimes your father and Jack came to blows and the police had to be called on at least one occasion. They made up but then your father was killed in a car crash. You and Jayne were simply the products of that very complicated four-way relationship. In fact there had been whispers quite early on that your father was also Jayne's real dad. It later came to light that Big Jack couldn't have children and he actually knew that Laura was pregnant with your father Lionel's child. Big Jack told us that it was all to do with a growth he had in his lower regions. People were always going to get hurt and I think he purposely allowed your father to have sex with Laura to help keep her sweet. That's why the rest of our family brushed it all under the carpet. To be honest it was disgusting and it was just easier not to speak about any of it!' she said.

It was all a bit weird and I felt aghast but wasn't really surprised but at least Amanda has now finally confirmed what really happened. I then told her about the incident at Brookwood Station and that my article could make it on to the front cover of the *Woking Tribune* soon, although it could be a few more weeks yet. I also told her that there may be a supernatural connection with Tommy.

'Don't be stupid, you don't believe in all that rubbish do you?' she laughed.

I could sense a mood change so just laughed and decided not to say anymore. She then asked if I had been speaking to someone called Missy in Knaphill. I hesitated and then remembered Hope Pengelley, the old lady I had met who was married to Tommy's best friend Donald.

'Yes, yes I have,' I said feeling rather shocked by the question.
'I've spoken to her on the telephone very recently,' she said.
'Why?'

'Well she phoned me actually and told me about your visit after she had managed to put two and two together.'

'How do you know each other?'

'She obviously knew your grandfather but eventually also got to know his brother Clifford and his wife Gloria very well. They're my parents of course!'

'Oh yes, sorry but I don't understand.'

'Hope Pengelley or Missy as some people call her is my God Mother. Apparently I was christened at St Mary's Church around the corner from here in Park Road. My christening shawl is still upstairs in the attic. Your mother wanted it for you but sadly you were never christened.'

I felt a sigh of relief as I don't do God and all that stuff but again I couldn't believe what I was beginning to hear. My life has been so full of co-incidences recently. Too many revelations as well I thought.

I was just about to leave when Amanda grabbed my arm.

'I had another visitor last night you know?'

'No I don't, who?'

'Your ex wife, Kazkia.'

'Ex? Well I'm not divorced from her yet. What the hell did she want?'

'She came round to see how I am. A courtesy visit as she called it but I think there's more to it than meets the eye. Be very careful, she appears to be up to something. I think she wants you back!'

I declined to reply but nothing surprises me with Kazkia anymore. People are beginning to see her for what she really is. Amanda could sense I was beginning to become quite emotional and told me to get myself a stiff drink on the way home. She popped a five pound note in my top pocket.

'There you go, drop by the pub on the way to get your bus and have a little one for me as well, and next time, don't ask me so many bloody stupid questions,' she said with a smile.

We hugged and gave each other the customary peck on the cheek before I left. Amanda didn't seem her normal self but I do think that she's quite relieved that I've now found out what happened with my father. It must be less of a burden for her to carry I thought.

7

As soon as I got into the office this morning Geoff was gesticulating at me.
'The old girl wants to see you straight away,' he said.
'Why?'
'I don't know, she's just been out and asked where you were.'
'But I'm not late; in fact I'm at least ten minutes early!'
'Don't shoot the messenger!' he retorted.
I knocked on Nancy's door.
'Come!' She shouted rather loudly.
I entered and sat down in the usual chair.
'Do we have a problem?' she asked and then paused.

The pause was only for a few seconds but it seemed to me like an eternity and I was thinking of all the worst case scenarios, please tell me that I didn't get her pregnant that night I went back to her house I kept thinking. The blood rush was still happening when she suddenly stood up and walked over to the window.

'I met with Phil Janner yesterday evening just after you had left,' she said.

I felt an immense sigh of relief but didn't know what she was going to say next so I spoke out quickly.

'Why do you think we have a problem?' I asked.
'It's something he told me about you which bothers me,' she said.
'What?'
'Tell me about your grandfather'.

I felt aghast and then realised that Phil must have said something about Tommy and that there could be a connection between him and the incident at Brookwood.

'What do you want to know?'
'I need you to tell me what's going on, I'm confused and I don't like being surprised with this kind of stuff.'
'What kind of stuff?'

Phil told me that you think that there is a possible connection between your grandfather and the ghost of a young lady who died in

1931 who just happened to want to come back to life and throw herself under a train again, am I understanding this right?'

'Err, well sort of.'

'Be specific please and tell me what this is all about.'

'Over the past few weeks I have been researching my family tree. Initially to find out what had happened to my father but then my aunt let me have some old keepsakes she had of my grandfather's. He died four years ago but had a remarkable life so I've been trying to find out more.'

'So how does this all connect with what happened at Brookwood Station?'

'Over a couple of weekends I visited some people in Knaphill to find out more about Tommy's time in the asylum over there. It's in the process of being closed down so I thought I would get over there and try and find out as much as I could before it was too late. I met with an old lady called Hope Pengelley who remembered my grandfather and a lot of what she told me matched the information that he had written down in his diaries. There are three diaries from 1929 to 1931. He mentions a lady called Maisie who was killed by a train on the 13th July 1931, that's the same date as our incident at Brookwood occurred.'

'So how is your grandfather connected to this Maisie lady?'

'They were lovers; Mrs Pengelley told me all about them. There was some confusion over Tommy's whereabouts and Maisie ran off down to the station and jumped under a train,' I said.

'So you are telling me that the driver of the train at Brookwood actually hit a ghost!'

'Yes, Reverend Bream has his own views but explained the paranormal angle to me as he sees it and Esther the psychic medium told me that the spirit of Maisie was watching over me because she's still searching for Tommy on the other side.'

'This all seems a bit far-fetched to me and I find it unbelievable that you think that there's a connection between the incident and something that happened in your family all those years ago. Quite frankly I find it quite pathetic.'

'Pathetic it certainly is not,' I said rather angrily.

Nancy paused again. She went to the door and shouted out to Beryl to make two coffees.

'Tell me about that hospital place you went to.'

'Why?'

'Well you obviously need more help, your imagination is getting the better of you and I don't want it affecting your work. You are showing signs of becoming a very good reporter and I'm trying to assist you here as best I can.'

'Look, I don't need help. There are three people now who actually agree that the incident at Brookwood is linked with the death of Maisie in 1931. Phil Janner has confirmed the dates; the Reverend Bream has given me his views on the phenomena and Esther who you brought into help in the investigation has told me about the presence of a spirit following me around. I haven't just made all this up!'

'Okay, sorry, look. I'm just very confused and part of me wants to drop the whole thing now. If readers know that one of our own reporters has personal links to the story it may potentially compromise our integrity as a community publication and I won't have this paper put in a position like that.'

'That's exactly why I didn't mention the personal aspect before and kept it out of the story. The incident at Brookwood the other week happened anyway so it does need to be investigated further. There is no need for me to mention that I or members of my past family are involved.' I said.

'But what if Reverend Bream decides to report on your family connection in his article for the *Fortean Times*, you didn't think about that now did you?'

'No I didn't but I don't think he will anyway; he seems a bit sceptical.'

'Well he won't because I've already spoken to him.'

'What did he say?'

'His article is just about to go to press and he's taken your details out and replaced them with something which is a bit more colourful and alternative to say the least. He owed me a favour from a couple of years ago. I can't afford for a member of *Tribune* staff to be cited or named in the magazine, not with that kind of story and definitely not with Mr Hackett breathing down my neck all the time. Many people see the magazine as satirical rather than one about the paranormal anyway and if Reverend Bream can manipulate the truth so easily then that proves it!'

The Reverend Bream won't want to hear that I thought.

'So what shall I do now?'

'Carry on but remember there is other news and I don't want this taking up all your time. I want to see a completed feature article with the other bits I asked for within the next two weeks explaining exactly what happened and any real evidence to support that would be beneficial. Can you do that for me?

'Yes, of course and there won't be any personal slant, that's all my own business anyway,' I said.

'Good. Just keep me informed of any developments about this spirit lady but I will be ringing Esther shortly, I want her to tell me what she's told you if just for my own peace of mind. Would you have a problem with that?

'Err no, no problem at all,' I said.

After I left Nancy's office I went back to my desk and just stared at the ceiling for a couple of minutes.

'Are you alright?' Lisa asked.

'Yes, fine I think.'

Just then my phone rang.

'Esther here, how are you?'

'That's weird; I've just been in Nancy's office talking about you,'

'I know, she just phoned me and asked me to tell her about Maisie. Is it alright for me to tell her now?'

'Yes of course, I assume she thinks that I'm going off my head again and anything you tell her will help now I think.'

'Okay thank you. I'll ring her back. Good luck with the rest of the feature by the way.'

'Thank you.'

Lisa was hovering behind me and trying to work out what was going on but I made my excuses and went off to the toilet. Safe in there for awhile I thought!

When I got back to my desk both Geoff and Lisa told me that my phone had been 'red hot' while I was in the loo.

'This lady is asking for you to contact her urgently,' said Lisa.
Carol on a 0252 number. That's Farnham. That must be Carol from the *Farnham Herald* I thought. After about five attempts I eventually got through.

'Hello Carol, this is Jack from the *Woking Tribune*.'

'Oh Hi Jack. Thanks for phoning back. Would you be able to come over to Farnham around eleven tomorrow morning?'

'I should be able to, why?'

'I've managed to get an interview arranged with Steve.'

'Steve?'

'Yes, Steve Callion the train driver. He's agreed to meet us at his house so he can tell his side of the story.'

'Ah, that's brilliant, thank you, of course I'll be there.'

'Okay, I'll meet you at the station and then I'll drive you up and we'll interview him together if that's Okay with you.'

'Of course it is, my train back down from Woking gets in about 10:47, is that Okay?'

'That's fine, see you tomorrow.'

When I put the phone down I leant back in my chair and let out a great big yelp. Nancy was standing behind me and the others were just staring.

'What's that all about?' Nancy asked.

'I've got a meeting with that train driver who was involved in the Brookwood incident tomorrow.'

'Good, hopefully he may give us a better idea of what really happened that night.'

'Exactly, exactly,' I replied rather enthusiastically.

I noticed that Lisa was still hovering. I think that she's a bit jealous that I'm on to my first big story and I wouldn't put it past her to try and worm her way in somehow and try and steal some of the credit, that's the sort of person she's become lately. She's quite devious and selfish and is becoming a bit of a back stabber and I feel that I can't trust her anymore. It's definitely time to keep my cards close to my chest as far as she's concerned I think!

8

It was rather frustrating having to travel up to the office just to check my in-tray and then come all the way back to Farnham to meet Carol this morning. Geoff is there and could have checked it for me, he knew I had this appointment today but he never wants to help. It's always 'Self,' 'self,' and 'self' with him and there was nothing in it anyway. No lie in for me his morning and a wasted journey which made me feel quite angry.

On top of that, it's very hot this morning and Carol was about fifteen minutes late, in fact I wondered whether she was going to turn up at all but then she appeared all in a fluster.

'Sorry I'm late, I've been trying to resuscitate one of my goldfish,' she said.

'What?'

'Well actually it's a Koi carp, one of our prize-winning fish; it was swimming around on its side when I went down the garden at first light to do the normal feed, it had been attacked by a heron I think.'

'Will it survive?'

'I don't know, it's lost a few scales and appeared to be in shock. You get to know how fish behave under certain circumstances after awhile you know.'

I tried not to laugh but I think Carol detected that I was quite amused because I couldn't help smiling. At least she didn't say anything.

'Right, now about the train driver. His name is Steve Callion and he lives in Haven Way in the house at the top. We'll drive up but you'll have to hold tight and enjoy the ride, all my friends tell me that I'm a bit of a Nigella Mansell when I get behind the wheel,' she joked.

Carol's car is an old grey Austin Cambridge, if it had a turret on the top it would look like a tank. When we got to Haven Way we both got out and walked up a long path until we got to a light blue front door. Carol rung the bell and a lady answered.

'Good morning can I help you?'

'I hope so, we've come to meet with Mr Callion, I'm Carol Drinkwater from the *Farnham Herald* and this is my colleague Jack Compton from the *Woking Tribune*'.

'Two reporters from two different newspapers at the same time, well we must be honoured. Oh, sorry, I'm Steve's mother, my name is Iris, Steve's out the back on the conservatory enjoying the sun and tending to some tomato plants for me.'

We walked through the house until we got to the conservatory. Steve stood up and shook our hands. I couldn't help noticing his pale pallor; he looked like he hadn't seen the light of day for months although I knew he had.

'So you've both come to talk to me about the incident,' he said.

'Yes,' Carol replied.

'Sorry, I'm Jack from the *Woking Tribune*, I understand you know Carol already.'

'Well we've spoken on the phone a few times but this is the first time we've actually met in the flesh.'

'Steve, what can you tell us about the night of the 13th of July?' Carol asked.

'At first it was just like any normal shift. I signed on here at Farnham at 16:05, read my notices and then worked the 16:35 up to Waterloo. I then worked the 17:52 Alton down and then back up to Woking where I had my PNB.'

'PNB?'

'Yes, physical needs break.'

'What then?'

'Things were a bit up the shoot and my next train was delayed so the TCS asked me and Bill Ashcroft the guard to work a set of empties down to the shed. It had a broken shoe-beam so was taken out of service.'

'What time was that?'

'20:39, we ran it as an eight car because the other unit couldn't be detached for some reason. I seem to remember that we were on yellow signals as soon as we left Woking. Normally it would have been green lights all the way.'

'By shed do you mean the depot at Farnham?' Carol asked.

'Sorry yes, we have nicknames and abbreviations for everything on the railway,' said Steve breaking into the smile.

'So what happened when you thought you hit somebody at Brookwood,' I asked.

'I know I hit someone and I still believe that despite what people are saying.'

'Can you please describe exactly what happened?' Carol asked.

'Well it all occurred quite quickly. I saw someone jump down on the tracks from the London platform, a young girl I think, she then ran over to the downside right into my path and then there was a sickening thud. I'd already slammed on the brakes by then but it was too late. All I remember after that was Bill coming through to the cab to find out what had happened. A couple of passengers shouted across from the up-platform and asked if I was alright and that was about it until the police and the MOM arrived.'

'Up-platform?'

'London bound.'

'How do you feel now?'

'I feel helpless and still in shock really. It hasn't helped that no-one has found a body yet. They med-screened me straight away and everything was Okay but now the management think I'm some kind of attention seeker. They don't believe anything I've told them about that night.'

'Did you know that there were two witnesses who said that they saw someone run in front of your train,' I said.

'No I didn't, no-one's told me that.'

'Were these the two people I just mentioned?'

'Yes probably.'

'I'm trying to look into it all a bit more and see if I can get hold of at least one of them for an interview but it depends on whether I can procure any details from the police.' I said.

'Leave that to me,' said Carol. I know a couple of bent coppers who might be able to help,' she added with a wink.

'Have you any idea when you may be allowed back to work?'

'There's talk of me going back on light duties and helping out in the List Office at Woking.'

'List Office?'

'Yes, it's where all the rosters are done, they want me to run around and be a messenger for the list clerks and make sure all the daily stuff and late notices get posted at the depots. They cover Basingstoke, Farnham, Guildford and Woking depots from up there so at least I'll get round a bit and should be able see some of my workmates,' he added.

'Do you think you will ever drive a train again?' Carol asked.

'I don't think so. It might have been easier if they had found a body, that would have given me some kind of closure and I might have been able to cope with that. Being fucked over by my depot manager hasn't helped and they've really contributed to making me look like a fool.'

I told Steve that I had spoken to a couple of experts about the incident and that they were both trying to throw some light on everything but he too is sceptical about anything paranormal and told me that he never believes anything until he sees it. I suggested that he should look at this all with an open mind and quite surprisingly Carol agreed.'

'So what are you people going to put about me in your newspapers?' he asked.

'I'm looking at the personal element from your point of view. Jack here is looking at the wider picture on behalf of the *Herald's* sister paper the *Woking Tribune*. We will get to the bottom of this and if we can help give a full explanation of what happened that night then we will,' said Carol.

I nodded.

'I'm making some progress. Something very odd happened that night and I promise that you will be the first to know when I get all the answers,' I said.

Steve smiled and looked a bit relieved but I could sense that he still wasn't totally convinced. He then told us that he had to go and visit a shrink this afternoon.

'The railway's paying for it; I've got to see a woman called Deborah at Hill Place.'

That hit home. Hill Place is the hospital where I stayed when I had my problems a few weeks ago. I feel for Steve but if it's the same Deborah who counselled me he should be in good hands although for professional reasons I felt it best not to tell him of my own recent problems.

When we left Carol suggested that we should find a quiet pub somewhere and compare notes. We went to The Nelson Arms in Castle Street, I had only ever been in there once a long time ago, around 1987 or 1988 I think. There was a big fish tank containing a piranha and Carol kept trying to get it to nibble her finger. Fortunately it didn't.

'Don't worry, they're pretty safe on their own,' she said.

I reminded her that the time was ticking away and that I couldn't stay too much longer.

'I shouldn't even be drinking,' I said.

'Look, if you need any help in writing any of this Brookwood story up, just give me a ring. Don't worry, our articles are going to be totally different, for one thing, I don't believe in the paranormal element to all this and I'm only going to do my write up based on Steve's personal suffering and the disruption the whole incident caused.'

'But do you think he's off his head?' I asked.

'That young man definitely needs help but something did happen that night and as you say, there were two witnesses and it would be really helpful if we could talk to them.'

I looked at my watch again and thought I'd better make my way back up to Woking if only to show my face and give Nancy some feedback about this morning's meeting so I thanked Carol for all her help and we said our goodbyes. At the station I got some mints so I could hide the smell of the alcohol, it was only one pint but I can always smell it on Geoff when he's had a few so I thought it best not to take any chances.

When I returned to the office Geoff was the only one there.

'Oh, the wanderer has returned, maybe I can fuck off now,' he said with a grin.

'Where are all the others?'

'They're over the pub, it's the old girl's birthday and she's having a bit of a shindig. She's also happy that Hackett has given the Okay for her holiday as the circulation figures are up. Something to do with that business down at Brookwood the other week,' he said.

'Oh, by the way there's loads of stuff in your in-tray now,' he added.

I sifted through the tray and there was a full report from Reverend Bream about his take on the incident at Brookwood Station. There was also a note saying I could use his material to support any feature article I was writing as long as I gave due acknowledgement to him and mentioned the *Fortean Times*. Another note was from Nancy inviting me over the pub. I decided not to go.

9

I was the first one in the office this morning so decided to make myself a coffee. Just after I sat down Ted, and then Beryl appeared. I got up and offered them both a cup.

'Yes please, strong one,' said Ted.

'Strong for me too, very strong and plenty of sugar,' Beryl requested.

They then sat down but didn't say too much until Ted announced that he had a hangover. Beryl admitted having a bit of one too, her first for about ten years apparently. I noticed that it was getting on for 10 o'clock and there was still no sign of anyone else which was very unusual.

'You should have come over last night, I think Nancy did leave you a note,' said Beryl.

'Yes I saw it but decided against going over; I just wanted to get home to be honest.' I replied.

'Coward! You missed all the fun, it was one hell of an evening, Geoff was incredibly pissed and was falling over everywhere,' said Ted.

'He was bad, very bad as well as embarrassing,' added Beryl.

'Why what did he do?'

'When we first got there a young man walked in with a pretty little Chinese girl and Geoff asked him if he'd just been down to the takeaway.'

'Oh dear!'

'And if that wasn't bad enough he dropped a tray of drinks he was carrying for Mr Hackett and the lady who was with him got soaked, it went all over the place and the landlord wasn't very happy either,' said Ted.

'But I thought Mr Hackett was seeing Lisa?'

'So did we,' said Beryl 'but he walked in with a tall Scandinavian looking girl, probably Swedish, Lisa was mortified, broke down in tears and then stormed off. I went after her but couldn't console her so I just let her go home in the end.'

'Where was Nancy while all this was going on?'

'Oh that's another thing, she was in the corner snogging Dan most of the evening,' said Ted with a massive grin all over his face.

'Dan, who our Dan?'

'Yes, Mr Sports Journalist Dan.'

Beryl laughed and said, 'and that's not the end of it.'

'What do you mean?'

'Just as the pub was about to close Nancy's husband came to collect her, she'd obviously forgotten he was due to pick her up. She'd gone back to Dan's house by then. Her husband was furious and wanted to know where she'd gone but then Geoff butted in. He told him that she'd run off with you, got yours and Dan's names mixed up. He was so drunk it was all quite funny in the end really.'

'So does her husband think that she was with me last night then?'

'Probably, you need to be careful, he's built like a brick shit house, you'll need to watch your back with that one,' laughed Beryl.

Ted also laughed. Just then Nancy came through the door with a big smirk on her face and went straight into her office. Within minutes I could hear her shouting on the phone.

'She's probably having an argument with her husband,' Ted quipped.

'What's her husband's name?'

'Simon, I think.'

'Time to take cover,' said Beryl.

I decided to go back to my desk and get on with some work. There were a couple of new stories and also a message for me to contact Wilbur, the porter at Brookwood station. I decided to file the new stories first, a cake sale at the Pied Piper Nursery School in Knaphill and one about a little boy in Wych Hill battling leukaemia. I then felt a hand on my shoulder. I turned around and it was Nancy.

'A quick word in my office please,' she said.

'Why didn't you come over to The Albion last night?'

'I saw your note but I already had things arranged so I went straight home.'

'You missed a good night.'

'I heard it was eventful.'

'Yes it was and you could have had me again if you were there, I would have rather been with you than with that dreadful Dan. He just fell asleep on me when we got back to his place,' she said.

I tried not to laugh and just thought to myself that I had had a lucky escape.

'Did you know my husband is looking for you?' she asked.

'Yes, Beryl and Ted just told me; apparently it was something to do with Geoff.'

'He got you mixed up with Dan somehow. Anyway don't worry about it I'm getting shot of him again.'

'Who, Geoff?'

'No, no not Geoff, my husband, I just need to be loved and he never shows it, he's more interested in betting on the horses and the dogs than he is being with me.'

Now I was feeling very uncomfortable. Fortunately we were interrupted by a knock on the door from Beryl. I could hear whispers. Nancy asked me to leave her office.

'We'll talk later,' she said.

The whispering continued for awhile and through the partially opened door I could see Beryl putting her arm around Nancy who was starting to cry. I was trying to make out what was going on but then Nancy stood up and closed the door completely. I couldn't hear a thing after that. Ted looked at me a bit concerned and suggested that we both went out for a sandwich.

'I think something serious has happened,' he said.

We went over to the Sandwich Emporium and then sat opposite on the bench where the bus stops are. After awhile we decided to walk back.

'I think we need to brace ourselves when we walk back in,' he said.

Beryl was in the kitchen area washing up some mugs and beckoned us over. She looked like she'd being crying too.'

'What on earth is it?' Ted asked.

'It's young Lisa, she's on a life support machine at Frimley Park Hospital, she wrapped her car around a lamppost on her way home from the pub last night, things are not looking good. All we know is that her family are with her and are expecting the worst.'

Ted and I looked at each other and then sat down. I felt him tremble and I could feel a lump come into my throat. Everything seemed to go cold as if I was in some kind of shock. There was complete silence.

'Where's Nancy?' Ted eventually asked.

'She phoned her husband and told him what had happened and he came to collect her while you were both out,' said Beryl.

'What after all that crap we've heard this morning?'

'Yes, that's what their marriage is like, very fickle, one minute they're all over each other and then they're declaring war; it's always been like that with them two.'

'I do hope Lisa will be alright, do you think it had anything to do with Mr Hackett turning up with that other woman?' I asked.

'Almost certainly, she was well worked up and when she left she was in a terrible, terrible state.'

'Had she been drinking much?'

'Oh yes, quite a lot, she was on the G&Ts and when Mr Hackett and his lady friend turned up she went berserk and stormed out,' said Ted.

'Yes, yes, I spoke about that already this morning,' Beryl said.

'The only thing we can do now is wait and hope for the best,' she added.

On the train home I kept thinking about Lisa. Everything has happened very quickly with her since she joined the *Tribune* a few weeks ago. I wonder if Mr Hackett knows about what's happened with her yet. I wonder if he will care!

Note: I must remember to phone Wilbur in the morning.

10

The mood in the office was quite sombre this morning. Geoff was back in after being missing all of yesterday and was looking very subdued. Dan was about writing up his latest on the cricket at Guildford and Jasmine offered to make the teas and coffees for the first time since I could remember. We were all wondering about Lisa when Nancy came out of her office to make an announcement.

'I've just spoken to Lisa's father on the phone. She's still on the life support machine but she's made it through the night which is obviously a good sign. Her dad has told me that she has serious chest injuries and there has been a lot of internal bleeding. He is however hopeful that she will pull through and said that the next two or three days are crucial.'

'Poor girl, poor girl,' said Beryl who had just walked in.

'Bloody hell, how long has she been driving? I didn't even know she had passed her test,' said Geoff who had only just learnt of the accident.

'Apparently she only passed her test very recently,' Nancy explained.

Everything went quiet again which was strange as everyone was in the office today.

'Come on, back to work, its deadline day,' Nancy ordered.

After I'd cleared my in-tray I remembered to phone Wilbur at Brookwood Station. After about four attempts I eventually got through.

'Hello is that Wilbur?'

'Yes, Wilbur talking.'

'Hello its Jack from the *Woking Tribune*. I had a message to call you.'

'Hello, yes man, I have some news for you about that man whose details I gave you, you know, the witness.'

'Who, Reginald Smythe?'

'Yes, that's him.'

'He came through again the other morning just after the peak and asked me when the next train to Waterloo was, he had missed the last one by about three minutes so had a twenty seven minute wait as the one up from Basingstoke had been cancelled. I went back into my office only for a couple of seconds and when I went back out to the platform he was gone.'

'Maybe he changed his mind about travelling,' I said.

'No, no, there's more than that. He had a ticket and never went back to the ticket office downstairs to get a refund. My station manager was here shortly afterwards and I told him about the man. We have a new CCTV machine and I asked my manager to take a look. When he rewound it to the time the man was talking to me on the platform, there was only me there and it looks like I'm talking to myself. He was definitely there, I definitely spoke to him. My station manager poked fun at me and asked if I'd been drinking.'

'Okay, does your station manager know about the incident?'

'Oh yes, he knows about it but he was on annual leave when it happened.'

'What's his name?'

'John Willard.'

'Do you have a number for him?'

'Yes, go through our switchboard and ask for him on extension 8413.'

'Okay thanks; is there anything else you remember?'

'No man, that's it.'

'Okay, thank you for your time.'

When I put the phone down I wondered. Has Wilbur actually been talking to a ghost after all or is there a more rational explanation? I thought about phoning his station manager but felt he wouldn't be able to shed any light on the matter. I then thought about Tommy's diary and his entries about Reginald Smythe. I needed to do a bit of cross-checking and wondered if there's any mention of his death in our archives here at the *Tribune*. Geoff has been transferring the files to computer since he's been confined to the office so I need to ask him to find out where it's best to look.

'Geoff, if I wanted to find out about someone who died in the 1930s how can I look it up?'

'That's still on the fiche; I've only got up to 1924. I've still got another seventy years to go before I get everything across, I need some help with all of this but as far as Nancy is concerned each time I ask, my request falls on deaf ears.' he said.

'Well it might help if you actually came to work sometimes,' Beryl quipped.

I could see Geoff's expression changing for the worse so I offered to make the coffees to defuse the situation. I needed to stretch my legs anyway. Just then Nancy appeared.

'Be a love, here's my mug, can you make me a hot chocolate while you're there,' she said.

'Of course.'

'So how's this epic Brookwood story of yours shaping up?' she asked.

'Well it seems like we have our first ghost,' I told her.

'What?'

I told her about the conversation I had just had with Wilbur and at first she seemed quite excited but then her mood changed.

'No. Don't jump the gun. Wilbur maybe playing games, either that or he's just simply seeing things. Did you say you had his station manager's phone number?'

'Yes!'

'Then phone him and tell him what Wilbur has told you and see what he says.'

'Okay I will.'

I gave Nancy her hot chocolate and passed Geoff his coffee and walked back to my desk. Trying to get through on railway telephone numbers is always an arduous task and their switchboard couldn't connect me with John Willard but they did leave a message with someone asking for him to call me. I had only just walked away from my desk when the phone rang.

'Hello, can I speak to Jack Compton please?'

'Yes, this Jack, how can I help you?'

'I'm John Willard, station manager for Brookwood; I've had a message to call you.'

'Oh yes, thank you for getting in touch so quick, its most appreciated. I'm working on a story at present about an incident that occurred at Brookwood on the night of the 13th of July and I have spoken to your porter Wilbur White a couple of times.'

'Ah Wilbur…'

'I just need to verify a couple of things before I complete the article I'm working on and was wondering if you could tell me what he's like.'

'Wilbur is a good worker; he works at a slow pace but does manage to get things done. The public like him and he keeps the station down at Brookwood spick and span. He even comes in on his days off just to look after the flower arrangements down there. Yes, he's a very dedicated member of staff'.

'He told me that you helped him look for a passenger on the CCTV the other day but you couldn't find anyone.'

'Yes the equipment is new; to be honest I'm not really sure how to work it myself. The pictures are not very good, everything is very grainy. Wilbur did make me laugh; all we found was an image of him waving his arms about and talking to himself.'

'Has Wilbur got a tendency to make things up?'

'Oh yes all the time. He should be called Walter Mitty. Always dreaming and playing practical jokes, that sort of thing. That's why I didn't believe him when he told me that he thought he'd seen a ghost. I should send him for a medical really.'

'Right, Okay, thanks, thank you for your time, I appreciate your help.'

When I put the phone down I wondered if it was worth pursuing the Reginald Smythe angle any further, Nancy was right to make me challenge Wilbur's version of events but I still have the note he gave me with Reginald Smythe's details on. Each time I've tried to the call the number it's unobtainable and Directory Enquiries has since informed me that the number doesn't exist which is a bit strange. Is the note in Wilbur's handwriting or is it that of Reginald's?

Back home I was able to think things through a little more. I decided to revisit Tommy's diaries to see if I could find out more about Reginald but there was nothing I hadn't already seen. The one thing that intrigues me is why is it Reginald Smythe, a man who was apparently at Brookwood Asylum at the same time as my grandfather whose name keeps cropping up? Wilbur could not have known anything so he's definitely not playing any practical jokes on anyone this time despite what his station manager might think. I think I will pay Wilbur another visit on my way to work in the morning even if it is at the risk of having to drink another cup of his horrible tea.

11

Brookwood Station was very busy this morning. Trains were delayed and there were a lot of troops from Pirbright on the platform with all their backpacks and gear waiting to go home for the rest of the summer holidays. Other new recruits were arriving and there was a colour sergeant on the steps barking at them to get on a big white bus outside on the forecourt. Wilbur was running around like a blue ass fly trying to appease people. I had to admire him for his resilience even if at times his comments were a bit crass.

'When's the next train to London due?' one lady asked.

'I'm not a Jew, I'm Rastafarian,' he replied with his strong Caribbean accent.

I had to laugh!

Eventually after about an hour when things had calmed down he invited me into his office.

'Tea?'

'Err, no thanks.'

'Coffee?'

'Err, no, thanks anyway but I'm not really thirsty at the moment.'

'Okay, I get the hint, you don't like drinking my brew,' he laughed.

I just smiled.

'What can I do for you today?'

'I need to know more about Reginald Smythe. I believe you actually did see him.'

'I'm glad you do, no-one else seems to believe me.'

'Do you think you've actually been talking to a ghost?'

'I wondered that. When I was a little boy back home my mother said that I was always talking to myself. I thought I was actually talking to my grandmother.'

'What's was wrong with that?'

'My grandmother died seven years before I was born.'

'Do you think you may be susceptible to spirit?'

'What does susceptible mean?'

'It means that you are likely to be influenced by or believe in something unusual or being open to an idea or something like that.'

'That all sounds very complicated but if you're asking me if I believe in ghosts then perhaps I do.'

'So, was the man you saw who said he was Reginald Smythe a ghost?'

'He looked very real to me at the time,' said Wilbur quite assertively.

'And what about the CCTV image that Mr Willard showed me, can you explain why there was no-one else there?'

'No I can't but I know what I saw and I gave you his details.'

'Did he write them down or was it you?'

'No, it was me, I just wrote down his name and number when he told me. When I looked up from doing that he was gone.'

I could sense that Wilbur was becoming very flustered and frustrated and was trying not to get angry so I decided to end the conversation. When the next train to Woking arrived it was already packed solid so I ended up standing in the guard's van. I looked up and recognised the guard; it was Bill Ashcroft who was on the train the night of the incident. I struggled through to talk to him.

'Remember me? I'm Jack Compton from the *Woking Tribune*.'

'Oh yes, I remember you. I heard that you and my friend Carol from the *Herald* went to visit Steve the other day.'

'Yes, that's right.'

'Did you get anywhere?'

'We're still looking into the incident but the railway management haven't been very helpful. They're quite sceptical about everything to say the least. We're looking into the incident a lot deeper and if we can shed any light on what really happened that night we will,' I said.

'Well if you need any more help with anything give me a shout; you know where to find me.'

'Thank you.'

When I arrived at the office Geoff was the only one there.

'Oh look here he is, late again!'

'Actually no, I've been interviewing someone at Brookwood.'

'Oh you're not still working on that fake suicide thing are you?'

'Fake suicide?'

'Yes the ghosties and ghoulies thing. It's about time you got used to the real world. You should leave it alone and start being a proper newspaper reporter. You should go and find something real to tell the world about.'

I was about to react but then thought that maybe he had a point. I had spent a lot of time on the story probably because of the personal connection. I now wonder if I have become too obsessed, too embroiled in everything. Just then the phone rang.

'Good morning, can I speak to Ms Salem please.'

It was a man's voice.

'I don't think she's here at present, can I help you at all?'

'Hello, I'm Lisa's father Howard Luscombe, I'm just phoning in with an update on Lisa.'

'How is she?'

'I'm relieved to say that she's now out of intensive care and on one of the wards.'

'Oh, that's great news!'

'Yes, we're very relieved. It's going to take some time, a few months probably. We thought we had lost her but she's going to be alright, we just need to give her a lot of love and support. With a bit of patience and hard work she should make a full recovery. She will just have to learn to live with her scars,' he said.

'Can you pass my message on to Ms Salem?'

'Yes of course, please give Lisa my best regards.'

'Sorry, who have I just been speaking to?'

'Jack, Jack Compton.'

'Okay Jack, I'll pass on your message.'

'Who was that?' asked Geoff.

'It was Lisa's dad. She's going to be alright!'

Just then Nancy walked in and I told her about the call.

'Well that's good news, something to celebrate. I'll get Beryl to arrange a card and some flowers.'

'Oh not more frilly stuff,' quipped Geoff.

Nancy looked daggers at him and I tried not to respond but that was typical Geoff and he wonders why he's been refined to barracks as it were.

Once again, my in-tray was quite full and I was in the process of prioritising my work when I found a fax from Esther. She's the guest psychic medium at the Spiritualist Church in Camberley next week and has asked if I would like to attend. Perhaps I should. It might help me to understand more about the whole process of how people talk to the dead.

12

Meeting with Esther again has been something of a surreal experience. She wanted to meet me in the Carpenters Arms in Camberley before going off to the Spiritualist Church in Gordon Road.

'It's quite quiet in the early part of the evening so we can have a quick chat; this is where I used to come when I was courting about fifteen years ago. I was always in here, the Cambridge Hotel or up to no good in Ragamuffins, the night club,' she told me.

I told her that I used to live in Camberley as well and that Amanda still does but I don't think she was very interested in hearing about what I was trying to say. All of a sudden she seemed to be absorbed in something else.

'This pub is haunted. Can you feel it?'

I did feel a bit of a chill but wasn't too convinced so I asked her to explain.

'Remember, I told you before that many psychic mediums like me use a spirit guide to describe an entity that may be attempting to make contact with the living. With the help of a guide I can use my 'third eye' to see spirits, the images can then become full apparitions; they are vivid and appear very real. I can clearly see a couple who I think were previous landlords here, a priest, an old man sitting in the corner at the front by the window and two children in Victorian dress going through the door to get into what used to be a cottage next door.'

'Can you see them now?' I asked.

'Oh yes, it's all happening right before me, the images are very strong!'

Esther told me that she picked up her spirit guide a few years ago, a young child called Emma when she worked at the King Lud pub in Ryde on the Isle of Wight. Emma has stayed with her ever since. She believes that the girl had been murdered by a seven-foot tall poltergeist after hiding a wallet in the scullery at the pub.

'Whilst many people sense or feel the presence of a spirit, most will never see them. Communicating with the spirit world is a gift that I am blessed with and of course very happy to talk about. My 'third eye' is really my mind's eye. Behind my physical eyes there is an intuitive eye and I am able to use this for soul to soul seeing and that's how I think I can interact with the spirits right here in the pub.'

'Are you interacting with them now?'

'No not really. I'm talking to you but I believe that they can see me. The old man in the corner has already smiled and waved at me.'

'What do other people think about what you do?'

'Most people are totally oblivious to a ghostly presence, however if anyone should ever sense or see something or are perhaps even sceptical about their existence, I'm always on hand to happily talk and explain the phenomenon, at least from my point of view.'

I remembered that Esther had told me a lot of this before when we were in Enzo's wine bar in Woking. At least she was being consistent I thought.

When we got to the Spiritualist Church there was a guy about my age. He had long black hair and a pointed beard and was wearing a long black leather coat.

'Come inside, grab some tea or a cup of orange, we have biscuits and home-made fairy cakes too,' he said rather effeminately.

Esther smiled, 'I love that guy, he's so friendly, he's always here when I come, I'm sure he's on a different planet.'

That made me laugh, I was just thinking exactly the same about her!

When we sat down I looked around. There were only five others in the audience and then Esther stepped up on to the stage.

'Welcome to Camberley, I am Esther Whitehawk, I used to live here when I was younger and now I live on the Isle of Wight although I spent some time living and working in London in between. Does everyone here believe in spirit?'

Only one person put their hand up.

'Anyone else?'

Gradually two others raised their hands.

'I have a young girl beside me. She has short fair hair and is wearing a pale yellow dress; it could be part of a school uniform. Does anyone recognise her?'

No-one responded.

'Let me help you a bit more. She counts to nine then stops and is showing me the letter 'J'. Does anyone here know of a young lady, Jane, June, Judy perhaps?'

Very slowly a lady put her hand up. She was one of those who hadn't responded before.

'Yes, I think I recognise her.'

'Your daughter or niece perhaps?' interrupted Esther.

'Yes niece, her name was Julie!'

'She is showing me her chest and then places her hand over her mouth then shows me her chest again.'

'That would be right,' said the lady.

Just then Esther said that she was losing her connection with the spirit.

'Julie came to me and told me that she wants to know that it was no-one's fault. She says she is in a good place now and is being comforted by her two angels.'

'Yes one would be my sister, Julie's mother and the other, my mother, Julie's grandmother.'

'Thank you so much,' said Esther.

After the meeting while we were drinking tea the lady explained to us that Julie had passed away after suffering an asthma attack in June 1966 when she was just nine.

'I remember that day like it was only yesterday. No-one could help her, it all happened so quickly, she'd been happy all day and seemed as right as rain until that happened,' she said.

I came away from the meeting feeling quite perplexed. The lady who originally appeared quite sceptical about everything was the only one there who could identify anyone. I think all the others were there simply out of curiosity but I think Esther was quite convincing. I shall keep an open mind about it all but at least now I do believe that there is some truth behind what she says. Maybe there is life after death after all!

13

There is only Geoff and myself in the office this morning. He's not the best person to confide with, certainly not with the story I'm covering. He thinks it's all a load of old tosh as he calls it.

'Coffee?' I asked.

'Go on then, can you make it black?'

'Another heavy night?'

'Yes but I'd prefer it if you didn't tell anyone.'

'Are you Okay? You don't seem yourself today.'

'Don't laugh and I'd appreciate it if you'd keep your opinions to yourself; I have my review meeting with Nancy this afternoon. I'm hoping she's going to let me out and about again. I miss the freedom. The problem is that I know that she's already interviewed a freelance and he's starting on Monday. I'm worried that his appointment may affect my chances.'

'What makes you think that?'

'Hackett came in the other day when I was sat here on my lonesome. He said that he wants the paper to champion local people a lot more than it actually does. He reckons there aren't enough stories which cover what Woking's residents are up to. "Too much politics and sport," he said. He wants the *Tribune* to become the people's paper as he put it.'

I could see that Geoff was very worried and I was struggling to give him the right answer.

'Maybe if the paper changes direction a bit then it will throw up more opportunities. That will mean extra work for all of us. Perhaps that's why they're bringing in a new freelance.' I said.

'I hope you're right, all this sitting around the office fucking around with the filing is really doing my head in. I need to be out and about in the fresh air, and yes before you say it, I will leave the pubs alone!'

I smiled and thought to myself, 'yeah right'.

'Oh and by the way, Lisa's dad called just before you came in.'

'She's being allowed home later today but the police are investigating the crash and want to do some interviews to find out what she was doing and who she was with before it happened. Her old man's expecting her to be charged with drink driving and he's very worried about it all. I think he just wants to warn Nancy about what's going on.'

Just then the phone rang. It was Nancy. Geoff laughed.

'Blimey, her ears must have been burning.'

'Is that you Jack?'

'Yes it's me.'

'How did your meeting go with Esther at the spiritualist church last night?'

'Err, very well, I found out quite a lot. It will certainly help with the story.'

'Make sure it does, we can't afford too much more time on this one. Mr Hackett told me yesterday that he wants to see a conclusion and the finished article in the paper next week. He also wants us to stop cavorting with the *Fortean Times* and the *Farnham Herald*, they don't pay us for the privilege and he thinks that they could be stealing our news.'

'Sorry, I thought that they were helping us rather than the other way around.'

'That may not be the case; they're reporters so they will be as shrewd and cunning as we are. Never trust another reporter. They will always be out to steal your story. Now, can you pass me over to Geoff?'

I grabbed the mugs and went to the kitchen to make the coffees. I could hear Geoff talking about the call he had received from Lisa's father and then he began to a whisper. I don't normally eavesdrop but on this occasion I'm curious enough to try and find out what's going on. After about twenty minutes I heard the phone go down and Geoff suddenly burst into song. It was quite weird, he's never done anything like that and I actually know the song he was singing, it was one Amanda always used to play a lot when I was young…

> *Ev'ry night I sit here by my window (window)*
> *Starin' at the lonely avenue (avenue)*

Watching lovers holdin' hands 'n' laughin' (laughin')
And thinkin' 'bout the things we used to do
Like a walk in the park
(Things) like a kiss in the dark
(Things) like a sailboat ride (yeah-yeah)
What about the night we cried?
Things like a lover's vow
Things that we don't do now
Thinkin' 'bout the things we used to do...

He sang it all the way through, it was certainly an unexpected piece of free entertainment.

'Well that's all off my chest at last,' he said.

'What do you mean?'

'Nancy has cancelled our meeting this afternoon. She's putting me back on normal duties with immediate effect; to say I'm chuffed is an understatement. After I told her about the call from Lisa's dad she's decided to go and pay them a visit this afternoon but she has asked everyone who was with Lisa before she left on the night of the crash to submit a report. It's just in case she gets asked any awkward questions by the police.'

'Do you think Lisa will be back at work soon?'

'Not if I had my way, she was playing up before the accident, besmirching us like we were just plebs. She's one of those who will gain your confidence and then once she feels comfortable with that, she walks all over you. I could see her doing it to both you and Ted and when she tried it on with me, I snapped. Well, you were here so you saw what happened. To be honest I don't want her back here but I wouldn't wish what happened to her on anyone.'

Today I've seen a lighter side to Geoff. I've actually enjoyed his company and been laughing with him nearly all day. I wish he was like that all the time. As we left the office I asked Geoff about the song he was singing.

'I'm a massive Bobby Darin fan, I love that song. It's one of my bath time favourites.'

I laughed.

'Pub?'

'Err, no thanks Geoff, I'll take a rain check on that one if you don't mind, By the way, I don't want to be making black coffees for you again tomorrow.'

'You won't have to. Beryl's back in the morning.'

I wandered off to the station. Now I need to focus on getting everything finished and I'll need to decide how to write it up and I'm really not sure what to do with it all next. I feel that the pressure is mounting…

14

Nancy was even more flustered than usual when she came into the office this morning. She looked very harassed.

'Okay you lot, my office five minutes sharp,' she demanded.

It was Ted's first day back from a few days off so Geoff was trying to bring him up to speed with the events of the last few days. Beryl was back and Dan was due in to fix his sports pages in time for the deadline. Jasmine has also made a rare appearance.

'Firstly thank you Beryl for making the coffees,' said Nancy.

'Yes we've missed you the last few days, the coffee has not been up to its usual standard,' quipped Geoff as he looked over and winked in my direction.

'Right, down to business and it's all quite serious. What I'm about to tell you does not go beyond these four walls otherwise we could all be implicated.'

'Implicated?' asked Beryl.

'Yes, implicated. I visited Lisa yesterday. She's now back at home with her family.'

'How is she?' asked Ted.

'Well she could have lost an eye, the socket is badly damaged and her vision is slightly impaired. She'll probably want to wear her hair down over her eye to cover it up. You know how vain she is. She also has a big hole in her chest where she hit the steering wheel and that will take some time to heal.'

'So how does what happened to her implicate us then?' asked Geoff.

'It's all about the lead up to the accident. Lisa is now claiming that Mr Hackett raped her at some point a few days before. To be honest I think it's more to do with the fact that he turned up in the pub with that Scandinavian woman. Mr Hackett and Lisa have obviously had sex and now I think she's trying to get one over on him. You know what she's like. When I visited yesterday her friend Trudy was there, she's a bit of a legal eagle and apparently she's given Lisa some advice on what steps to take next.'

'Is Mr Hackett aware of the allegation?' I asked.

'He will be. The police are going to interview him today. After that they may come here and ask you guys some questions. They'll be interested to know how Lisa was behaving before she left the pub and how much she drank. I don't think she was breathalysed on the night of the crash but they would have seen the blood test results by now from the hospital.'

'What will happen to the paper if Hackett gets banged up then?' asked Geoff.

'I'm not sure although I know he does have a business partner, someone who has invested a lot of money in the *Tribune* and he's listed somewhere as a non-executive director.'

'What does that mean?' asked Beryl.

'Don't ask me, I only edit the paper and manage you lot. I'm no good at all this business gobble-de-gook. I always leave that to the experts. Right, now you lot, back to work and remember what I said, not a word to anyone. Jack will you stay here for a minute please.'

Nancy asked me for an update on the Brookwood story and more about my meeting with Esther the other night. She wants me to revisit the station and talk to Wilbur again. She also suggested that I should have a further chat with Phil Janner the local historian in case he can throw any more light on what could be behind the story.

'I want you to make a mini-plan, a timetable which will demonstrate to me exactly what you're doing. If you don't have all the answers to finish the story by the end of next week then we'll almost definitely have to shelve the item. That will be a lot of working hours lost and I will not be very happy. That will almost certainly reflect on next month's appraisal.'

'Appraisal?'

'Yes, your appraisal, I'll confirm the time and date with you a little later. Now fuck off out of my sight and get the bloody thing finished.'

That was Nancy at her typical best I thought as I left her office and went back to my desk.

'Everything alright?' asked Geoff.

'Yes fine, absolutely fine.'

'She's not trying to have her wicked way with you again is she?'

'Ha ha very funny, no of course not, she just wants me to get my Brookwood thing finished as soon as possible,' I said.

'Ghosties and ghoulies,' retorted Geoff taking the piss again.

I laughed as I thought he was going to burst into song again but then realised that he wouldn't today as too many of the others were about.

I decided to take a full lunch hour and went along to the canal to eat my sandwiches and give myself a bit of time to think. After about five minutes I heard someone call my name.

'Jack, Jack how are you? How are you doing?'

I looked up and saw it was Jayne. I immediately stood and we hugged. It all felt quite strange but at the same time I could feel a bond, a true feeling of family connection. I began to tell her about the story I was covering for the *Tribune* and we both got quite immersed in conversation.

'If there's anything I can assist you with let me know. I've got a big box of stuff in my loft at home, I'll have a look through and if there's anything there which I think might help you find what you are looking for I'll give you a ring.'

'Thank you so much but now it's time for me to go back to work and make my arrangements for the next few days, time to stop procrastinating and finally do something about getting results.' I said rather hurriedly.

Jayne laughed and walked with me part of the way back to the office. It was a great surprise seeing her today and I kept thinking about what was said. I wonder!

At home I've finally decided to work out what I know of my family tree based on what Amanda has told me and what I can find in Tommy's old diaries. It looks more like just a branch than a tree but I'm hoping Jayne may be able to help me fill in some of the gaps one day…

Jack Compton
(1966-present)
|
Lionel Compton (1938-1966) - Rachel née Noble (1941-1970)
|
Thomas (Tommy) Compton (1905-1990) - Katherine née Clarke (1904-1949)
|

Jayne O'Leary (half sister)
(1966-present)
|
Lionel Compton (1938-1966) – Laura née Dombrowski (1940-1987)

15

Today I need to put all thoughts of my family tree to one side and try and work out how to finish the article for the newspaper. It feels that Nancy is even under more pressure from Mr Hackett now considering everything that's been going on. I need to look again at all the information I obtained from Phil Janner and Wilbur at the station. I've looked back through my interview notes with the traincrew and have examined the railway Control Log again. All the evidence, if I can call it that is pointing towards a paranormal episode from somewhere in history being repeated.

Phil Janner has given me all me the dates with one date, 13th July 1931 in particular standing out and Wilbur is one-hundred percent convinced that he's had an encounter with a ghost. The Reverend Nathaniel Bream from the *Fortean Times* has explained his theory on various paranormal connections and Esther is convinced that I am being followed by the spirit of Maisie who I now believe was the person killed at Brookwood Station in 1931. To make the story credible I somehow need to prove it all. My family connection is making me nervous and I'm still trying to figure out a way of leaving myself out of it without diluting too much of the story. One of the things which are confusing me is the so-called ghost of Reginald Smythe if indeed that's who he is. Why is he making an appearance at the station and what connection if any, did he have with Maisie?

I decided to take myself down to Brookwood by train to have another look around on my own. After I had alighted and the train had left the station everything became quiet. All I could hear was the hiss of electricity from the third rail and the cackle of crows and magpies coming from the cemetery. I walked over to the other platform and then looked at where the incident was supposed to have occurred. Momentarily I thought I saw a figure but then it disappeared but it did look remarkably like the description of Reginald Smythe that Wilbur had given me before. I wasn't sure and I wondered if it was just my mind playing tricks. I went around to the office to see Wilbur but another man was on duty today.

'Good afternoon, I'm Jack, Jack Compton from the *Woking Tribune*; I was hoping to find Wilbur so I could have a quick chat.'

'It's the lazy little bastard's day off today, can I help you mate,' he said rather gruffly.

'I'm still working on a story about the incident here the other week where a train driver thought he hit someone but a body was never found.'

'Oh that, yes everyone's still talking about it. I thought that Wilbur had made it all up but I was talking to my old mate Bill Ashcroft who was the guard on the train and he says it's all true. I don't know what to make of it.'

'Do you know anyone else who might know anything?'

'I suggest you walk over the forecourt to the Brookwood Hotel, that's been the only topic of conversation over there for the last few weeks, they've all got their own take on what happened, you're bound to find someone in there who can tell you something. I would walk over and have a pint with you but I've heard my manager's about so I'd better stay here. We're not supposed to drink on duty. Tin-tack and all that.'

'Tin-tack?'

'Yeah, tin-tack; instant dismissal mate!'

I went over to the pub and walked up to the bar. I noticed that there were two bars, a posh one with carpets and another with just lino and a pool table. Some old men were playing darts. Just then I heard a voice behind me. It was Phil Janner.

'Hello, young man, didn't know you frequented this place!'

'I don't normally but the chap working on the railway station said that if I popped in here I might be able to find out more about what's behind the incident we've been investigating.'

'Yes I've looked into that a lot more too. I suggest you push all this paranormal rubbish to one side. There has to be a logical explanation and I actually have a theory.' He said.

'Theory?'

'Yes, theory!'

'What?'

'I think that someone armed with some historical knowledge such as information about what happened in July 1931 is playing a

155

practical joke. I think that there may be two of them, a couple. One is a woman who dressed up in a white costume and pretended to jump in front of a train and the other, a man who is walking around the station platforms in broad daylight pretending to be a ghost.'

'It's feasible I suppose, but the train driver said he heard a thud.' I said.

'The woman could have thrown something at the train. Because of where the driver was sat in the cab he wouldn't have seen that, he would have seen her from a distance and then assumed he had hit her.'

'… and what about the man on the platform who I think is Reginald Smythe?'

'This is why I think someone is playing a practical joke. A man called Reginald Smythe committed suicide at the old asylum by drowning himself in a well. There was no recorded connection with him or Maisie. She died under the train a year or two later.'

I remembered that Phil had spoken to Nancy behind my back about my family connection with the incident and I wasn't sure about his integrity anymore.

Just then he asked me a bit more about the diaries.

'Can you remind me what was in those old diaries about the incident?' he asked.

I felt obliged to tell him.

'My Aunt Amanda gave me all of Tommy's old diaries; three of them were found in a tin and are from his days at the asylum. They clearly record what happened on the night of the incident and his feelings for Maisie and his anguish when she died. He even tried to see her body in the mortuary but an attendant there told him that he couldn't because it was all in bits.'

'Along with what I already know that's all very interesting,' said Phil.

'One of the things I'm always doing is digging out old burial records, this Maisie Albright is buried somewhere near Farnham, I believe her family may have lived over that way,' he added.

'Yes they did and Maisie is buried in a churchyard in Tilford.'

'Tilford, that's a quaint little place, I used to play cricket over there about twenty years ago. We used to go in the Barley Mow pub on the green and drink pints and pints of Directors bitter and play bar-billiards and shove ha'penny and then drive back here. It was naughty but they were good old days, halcyon days as we still call them.'

I told Phil that I was thinking of going over there one day to visit the grave to see if I could find any real answers. Phil laughed.

'You won't. All you'll do is freak yourself out and then come away even more confused. Stick to the logic. I've told you my theory and I suggest that's the only thing that you should consider when you come to finish your story. In my experience if you're not totally sure, ask the question yourself and let the reader come up with their own answers. Readers will always engage, I always do when I see something like that and it might help to sell more copies of the newspaper and that I imagine will please your editor and gain you some brownie points.'

I laughed.

'Thanks Phil, that's sound advice. How do you know all this?'

'Let's just say that I once dabbled in journalism, I'm retired now but I do still take an interest particularly if something has an historical edge. Also, I will be contacting you soon, I'm writing a local history book so I could do with bit of free publicity.'

I laughed again. 'Yes, I'll see what I can do,' I said as I made my way back over to the station.

16

Nancy was waiting for me when I arrived at the office this morning. Geoff had already gone out to investigate a burst water main that had flooded some homes in Horsell over night.

'Beryl, can you do the honours with the coffees please?'

We went into Nancy's office and she shut the door.

'Okay, I told you about Mr Hackett. He's been in touch and he's informed me that he's been released without charge. In fact the pendulum is swinging quite heavily in Lisa's direction. She was charged with drink driving and you won't believe this, driving while not qualified.'

'Not qualified?'

'That's right; she hasn't passed her driving test.'

'She told us that she had passed her test, I remember her celebrating,' I said.

'It was a lie and to top it all, police are also considering charging her with wasting their time and making false accusations. Mr Hackett never raped her and Lisa has now admitted to making the whole story up. He's told me to sack her but then we have another problem.'

'What problem?'

'Lisa's friend Trudy, the legal eagle I told you about works for the same firm of solicitors that represents the *Tribune*. She's also William Arrowsmith's daughter and he's one of the senior partners there. Mr Hackett is making arrangements to change our solicitors this morning. He's not going to want any further complications and he wants all this brushed under the carpet as soon as possible.'

'When are you going to sack her?'

'She's still too ill to come to work at the moment and of course there are the moral issues to consider. We are placing an ad for a replacement in this week's paper but Mr Hackett is having second thoughts about that, particularly as the new freelance has just started. It's all an extra burden on costs and the budget is very tight. We can only afford to pay the freelance £10.00 a story; he's not even on a salary so consider yourself lucky.'

Just then Beryl entered the office with the coffees and Nancy went outside for cigarette,

'Wait there,' she said, 'I still need a word about something else.'

I think she wants to talk about the Brookwood story. At least I know which way I'm going with it now, which angle to take. I think my chance conversation with Phil Janner yesterday may have helped me out a lot!

'Right young man, when are you going to take this old bird out for a drink again?'

I felt myself shudder and slowly sink down in to my seat.

'Don't worry, I'm only playing with you again, I know I frightened the pants off you last time,' she said.

Literally I thought. Part of me thinks that she may be testing the water to see how I would react. There is no way in the world I will ever want to sleep with that woman again.

'Seriously, I need to know how you're getting on with the Brookwood thing, I'm expecting the finished article to appear on my desk pronto,' she said.

I told her about what happened with my little trip down to Brookwood on the train yesterday and that I met again with Phil Janner. I mentioned his theory and that he seemed to think it was all some kind of elaborate practical joke.'

'Why on earth would anyone want to play a trick like that?' she asked.

'I don't know, it doesn't make sense but I think that the people behind it must know an awful lot about Brookwood Hospital and its history. If what Phil is saying is true then they must have had access to the hospital's old records.'

'Good thinking, you need to find out where all the patient records are, the old asylum is in its death throes at the moment and as you've seen, a lot of it has already been demolished. I have a hunch that it could be some hospital staff trying to have one last laugh but we need to find out why? I would get yourself back round there and ask a few more questions, I think we could be on to something at last.'

I noticed the way that Nancy was using the 'we' word now it seems I might be getting somewhere with the story and that bothers me a bit. I wonder if she might try and take all the credit when the article's finished. Now I wonder if I'll ever see my name on the front page, I suppose I will just have to wait and see although when I spoke to Ted the other day he said if I can crack it, it will be the biggest story the *Tribune* has had since the big storm a few years ago.

I decided to walk around to the bus stop and catch the No. 34 bus to Knaphill. I got off at the village centre, walked along the High Street and then into the Broadway and then past Almond Villa, the old farm bailiff's house. I remember Lisa talking about it when she was telling me about her great-grandfather. I walked down towards the old chapel. There were some builders sitting down eating their sandwiches and a huge bonfire burning away in the background. I walked around to one of the larger buildings, the one with the clock-tower; people were busy moving large crates of stuff so I decided to walk over to speak to a man who was wearing green overalls.

'Sorry, I know you're all busy, I'm Jack Compton from the *Woking Tribune*, I'm just trying to find out what's happening with all the old patient's records from here.'

'Oh, you need to go over to the Clerk and Attendant's office, look, it's just over there, you're lucky though, they're moving out tomorrow and everything will be gone.'

I walked over, all the doors and windows were open and there were lots of boxes and crates in the hallway.

'Anyone here?' I shouted.

'Yes, wait one, wait one I'll be down in a sec,' a woman's voice answered.

After about five minutes a woman in her forties finally appeared.

'Busy, busy. What can I do for you young man?'

'Hello, I'm Jack Compton from the *Woking Tribune* and would like to ask a couple of quick questions.'

'Good, I could do with a break, would you like a coffee? I don't have any tea.'

'A coffee will be fine, thank you.'

'Right, what can I do you for?'

'I need to know what will be happening with all the patient records now that the hospital is closing.'

'What for?'

'I've been investigating an incident which took place on the evening of 13th July at Brookwood railway station. There is an allegation, if not a possibility that some old records were used in order to restage a suicide which took place there on the same date in 1931.'

'That's very interesting because that's the year we've been looking to file and the records between March and September are all missing. One of my colleagues has blamed the Shadow-Masters.'

'Shadow-Masters?'

'They were a group of auxiliary staff who worked here at the hospital until about ten years ago. They formed a secret sect; it was a bit like a Free Mason's society. They used to meet in the crypt under the chapel until they were found out. Gradually they all dispersed and the group disbanded. No-one really knew who was in the group; it was all a bit weird.'

'Do you think that any of these people may still be around and would want to be involved in a hoax to mimic a real event which happened all those years ago? I asked.

'Anything's possible. Some of the staff here used to be as crazy as the patients, some still are. I wouldn't put it past anyone to do something like that. Please just don't ask me who though.'

'Sorry, I didn't catch your name.'

'I never told you, it's Wendy Rance, affectionately known to most of my colleagues as Bendy Wendy.'

I laughed.

'Do you know what's happening with the old patient's records and where they might be going?'

'There's a storage facility at Farnham Road in Guildford. There was talk of everything going to the council archive but Woking Borough Council have a reputation for throwing everything away and the powers that be wouldn't hear of it. Anyway, I must get on now,' she said.

I thanked her for her time and for the coffee and walked back to the village to catch the bus back to Woking.

Back in the office I decided to search the fiche machine to see if I could find out anything about the Shadow-Masters but there was nothing. I even looked through all the encyclopaedias on the shelf but again, no record of anything, no reference to them at all. It must have been some kind of made up name. Just then Ted came into the office.

'Hello Jack, you look a bit fed up,' he said.

I laughed and told him what I had been looking for.

'Shadow-Masters? I'm sure I've heard that term before. I remember covering a story a few years ago. There had been some strange goings on at Brookwood Cemetery around the pauper's plot. A huge cross had been set on fire and a mannequin which had been stolen from a charity shop was found hanging in a tree. Some sort of occult gathering had taken place. Among the ashes in the fire were some old records from the asylum, or hospital as it's known now but there was also a reference to Shadow-Masters, it was carved out on a piece of wood and left at the scene but no-one knew what it meant. I certainly couldn't follow it up as no-one would talk about it at the time. It was if people were too scared.'

That's interesting and I told him everything that Wendy had told me earlier.

'Well good luck but just stick to the facts when you write it up.'

Good advice I thought but like Phil Janner said, perhaps the article itself should ask a few of the questions!

The good thing about being busy at work is that it's helping me to forget about all the negativities that caused my illness. It actually feels like Kazkia and all that crap which went on with her is behind me now. It is a great feeling and I sort of feel liberated from myself. Tonight I've been looking through Tommy's old diaries again just to make sure that I haven't missed anything. There are so many references to Maisie; he was obviously so much in love with her. He must have felt really devastated when she was killed. What surprises me most is that he went on and had a distinguished career in the RAF but he never forgot her. I think he proved that when he visited her grave in Tilford when he came back that time for my father's funeral. I've decided that I would still like to go over to Tilford one day, perhaps after I've finished the story; just to pay my own respects.

Tomorrow I shall spend most of the day writing the article. I always like to leave the larger items on ice for a couple of days before submitting them to Nancy if the deadline permits, it gives me time to change anything if I have any second thoughts and of course more time to spot any errors.

17

I met the new freelance reporter today. He seems a bit of a shifty character; talks very softly but in short sharp and abrupt sentences. He was sitting at one of the hot desks and writing up his first couple of stories.

'Quite lucky this,' he said. 'An attempted murder and a rape in my first week, sorry, I'm Alfie, you must be Jack.'

'Yes I'm Jack and yes you are lucky, I've been waiting for a couple of stories like that to come my way ever since I've been here.' I said.

'Beginners luck, I call it,' he replied.

'Where did you used to work before coming here?' I asked.

'I worked at a lithographic printers in Aldershot but I got made redundant a few months ago. I then went and stayed with an old flame in Paris before coming back to look for a new job. So here I am.'

'I've heard you're not getting paid very well?'

'Working freelance for a local rag you never will. I got interested in journalism at university. I was there to get my maths degree but managed to switch my studies. That's where I got into writing. I ended up as editor of the campus magazine and also wrote bits for the National Union of Students papers. It was all quite exciting stuff.'

'Which university were you at?'

'Kent, the University of Canterbury to be precise.'

'Where did you go?' he asked.

'Nowhere, I just went to secondary school, I was sort of happy with that although to be honest I always hated school, I just ended up here by some kind of fluke,' I said.

I could tell he was a bit taken aback and he appeared to be looking down his nose at me. There was a kind of jealous, if not envious look in his eye so I decided not to say anymore. We seemed to enter into some kind of verbal Mexican stand-off.

'Coffee?'

'The perfect get out clause,' he said.

Well at least we both laughed.

I needed to go and find somewhere quiet to write up my story. Beryl suggested that as Nancy wasn't about until much later that I could go and use her office.

'She won't mind,' she said, 'and if she does you can blame me,' she laughed.

I went into Nancy's office and emptied my rucksack. I didn't realise how many notebooks I had got through. I had also brought Tommy's diaries with me just in case I needed to refer to anything. Although thinking about what Phil Janner said, they will probably be best left alone. I was just starting to plan my story and change my original draft when the door opened.

'Hello young man, what are you doing in here?' It was Mr Hackett.

'Err sorry, I was just using the office as I needed somewhere quiet to finish my story.'

'Sorry, you'll have to go back to your own desk, I will be using the office for the rest of the day while Ms Salem's out,' he said.

The office was quite noisy this morning. Everyone was in as they were getting everything formatted and finalised in time for the deadline.

Beryl came over, 'Sorry, he just walked through, there was no way I had time to warn you,' she said.

'Don't worry. It's just that I wanted to get my story finished today and I've got absolutely no fucking chance with all this racket going on,' I snapped.

'Steady, don't get so worked up about it. You don't need to swear. All the others cope when it's like this and you must learn to do the same.'

I told Beryl that I would go for a walk to try and recompose myself.

'Good idea, good idea,' she said.

I decided to walk around to Heater's Bakery and see if Jayne was there. She was, but she was very busy.

'Hey Jack, wait there,' She rushed from behind the counter and gave me a hug.' It's heaving right now, give me your number, I'll ring you later, perhaps you may like to come with me and Dave and the kids for a drink this evening before you catch your train back home.'

'Yes that would nice; I'll wait for your call.'

'Actually, just meet us here, it will be easier. 6 o'clock alright?'

'That's fine,' I said.

Talking briefly with Jayne had put me back in a good mood and I walked back to the office in a clearer frame of mind.

'Better?'

'Yes Beryl, much better,' I replied.

I went back to my desk and started sorting through all my notes and was able to build the new framework for my story. I wish I could do everything at home but it all needs to be done on the computer. Perhaps I could come back after I've seen Jayne and her husband. The office will certainly be much quieter then. The rest of the afternoon went quite quick.

I met with Jayne and Dave but there were no kids.

'We've left them at a friend's house; it's their eldest child's eighth birthday party. We're going back to pick them up at seven, so we've got about an hour. Let's go over to The Sovereigns pub and have a natter,' she said.

Dave seems very quiet and while Jayne was getting the drinks I got the impression that in some way he was sounding me out. He's Okay but not someone I would want to socialise with on a regular basis.

'There you go, pint of cider for you Jack, pint of lager for my fella here and one for me, happy days,' she said.

We all laughed.

Jayne then began to explain to Dave a bit more about our wretched past as she called it.

'Yes, our father was a bit of a one, look at the predicament that he's put us in let alone our poor mothers,' she laughed.

'Well at least you can both see the funny side of it all now,' said Dave.

I thought to myself, if only they knew the turmoil my upbringing had put me through, they wouldn't be laughing but then I remembered that Jayne is very much a victim too and she has her own way of coping with things. If it hadn't been for Amanda stepping in and looking after me when she did, I don't know where I would have been.

After three more quick pints it was nearly time to go. I was wondering if I would still be capable of going back to the office to write my story as I felt a bit tipsy.

'You'll be fine,' said Dave with a big grin on his face.

Jayne just winked at me with a little smile. We then said our goodbyes and I walked back to the station. I was still in two minds about what to do so I sat on the bench on the platform for awhile. I then noticed that my train was running about twenty-five minutes late, and that made up my mind for me. A quick coffee from the station buffet to help me sober up I thought and then back to the office. Surely, everyone must have gone home by now.

Walking up to the steps to the office I noticed a light come on. I could see shadows moving about in Nancy's office. I was now wondering if Mr Hackett was still in there so I waited and sat on the wall outside. I could now actually see two shadows so decided to move closer to the window. There was a crack in the blinds and it was getting darker outside. I could see that it was Mr Hackett and Nancy, there was a bottle of Jack Daniels on her desk and Mr Hackett was pouring the drinks into coffee mugs. After about five minutes he moved towards her and then I saw Nancy sink down to her knees. The desk was in the way so I couldn't see too much but I could guess what was happening. Mr Hackett's usually blank expression turned into a smile and then he let out a loud yelp that I could hear outside. Nancy rose to her feet, reached for her drink and then they kissed. I could see Mr Hackett readjusting his trousers. He then started walking towards the door and that's when I decided to make myself scarce.

I kept grinning to myself all the way home on the train and was thinking about what I had just seen. Probably best if I don't tell anyone about what I saw I thought. Most of all, I was disappointed that I wasn't able to get into the office and finish my story.

18

Geoff was buzzing around in the office in a total frenzy this morning going on about one of the stories he covered yesterday. He interviewed a 'young lady' who had been sexually discriminated against at the Latham's tool factory in Bisley and was dismissed on her first day in a new job.

He told us, 'When I got to her house the mother answered the door but when I met the person in question the immediate problem was that I couldn't tell if I was talking to a man or a woman. The mother then referred to her daughter as a post-operative transsexual. It's the strangest story I've had to follow up yet. Apparently the boss at the factory had called her a freak and told her to leave immediately when she turned up on her first day.'

'Post-operative, what does that mean?' asked Beryl.

'I think it means that the old todger's been chopped off,' Geoff replied with an unusual look on his face.

'Was it a transvestite or a hermaphrodite then?' Ted asked.

'No, I found out she was born a boy but does not want to be identified as a male anymore. She's only twenty-two but has had five or six sex-change related operations already. A transsexual is someone who has surgery to change their appearance and organs. She told me that she felt like a woman in a man's body. I did manage to find out that much,' said Geoff.

'What's her name?' I asked.

'Ashleigh or just Ash but I don't get it; I don't understand and besides all this is well out of my league. I have enough trouble dealing with this sort of thing when it's just a bloody poof!' Geoff laughed.

'Ooh-err!' shrieked Beryl.

'So did they tell her to leave just because of that, just because she wants to be different?' I asked.

'It may sound like that but when she went for the job she turned up dressed as a man and was interviewed as a prospective male employee. I inadvertently saw her copy of the application form and she had clearly put herself down as a 'mister'. It was only when she turned up on her first day at work wearing a yellow dress and red stilettos that it was clear there was a problem. The boss at the factory has used the lack of appropriate toilet facilities as his excuse for getting rid of her. That's why the mother contacted us with the story. I think that Ashleigh should have told the truth about her sexual identity in the first place.'

'That's probably not as easy as we can imagine,' said Ted with a sympathetic tone in his voice.

It was also quite odd to hear Geoff speaking so positively for a change but I think he knew he was on to a good story and wanted our support.

'Well Geoffrey, good luck with writing that one up, I look forward to reading it,' said Beryl as we all went back to our desks with a smile.

All these distractions are holding me up. At this rate I will never get my story finished. What doesn't help is that Alfie is already getting bigger stories than the rest of us and I can already see that he is quickly becoming Nancy's favourite; no doubt she'll be trying it on with him next. Just as I was thinking that, she came over to my desk

'Jack!'

'Nancy!'

'I assume you've been following up your information with updates from the British Transport Police and the railway haven't you?'

'I spoke to someone at the railway station a couple of days ago and I was planning to speak to the police this afternoon.'

'Make sure you do. It's important that you find out what they're doing if anything, I know the case is closed but check with them anyway, you never know! Who did you speak to at the railway?'

'I spoke to the chap working on the station at Brookwood. He's not the one I've been speaking to regularly, that's Wilbur but it was his day off.'

'I suggest you speak to someone at the railway press office and get an update from them. Their number is in our directory, you'll find it listed under British Rail.'

'I thought they were called Network Southeast now.'

'No, well, yes, but Network Southeast is just a brand of British Rail they use for this part of the commuter belt. I'm already working on a piece about the possibility of railway privatisation and how it will affect train services in the Woking area,' she said.

'Okay, thanks.'

I watched Nancy move away and start talking to Alfie. I thought I'd get up and make myself another coffee before sitting back down to make the calls. I'm trying to remember who it was who I spoke to last time at the Guildford BTP, hopefully I'll be able to find his name somewhere in all my notes.

'Ah, Good afternoon, could I speak to Sergeant Banger please?'

'Speaking…'

'Err, hello, this Jack Compton from the *Woking Tribune*, sorry for disturbing you, I was wondering if you could give me an update on the incident at Brookwood railway station on the night of 13/14th July?'

'Oh, yes, I remember that, I've spoken to you before haven't I?'

'Yes, yes you have.'

'Wait a minute; we have got something new, even though I think we closed the file.'

He seemed to take a long time coming back to me. I could hear voices in the background and the rustle of paper. It didn't help that the telephone was a bit crackly either.

'Hello, are you still there?'

'Yes I am,' I said.

'We closed the file a week after the incident because we believed the train driver had given us false information after suffering a mental episode. I believe he's now receiving medical help. We've also decided not to prosecute him at the request of the railway's solicitors and on the advice of our own prosecution department.'

'Did you say that you had something new?'

'Yes, one of my colleagues received a call only yesterday from someone who says he has a theory on the whole matter. He's gone over to Woking this afternoon to interview him.'

'That wouldn't be the Knaphill part of Woking would it?' I asked

'Well it sounds like you may be one step ahead of us,' he replied with a chuckle.

'So will you be re-opening the case if necessary?'

'No, but we could open a new one if we can prove that there was a trespass on the railway. I understand someone went on to the tracks in order to create the hoax and we would class that as a criminal act.'

'Okay, thank you for your time.' I said and put the phone down.

I decided to give myself a bit of time before phoning the railway. Geoff had just come back into the office.

'Malingering again?' he said as he observed me looking out of the window.

'No, just thinking.'

'... and you know what thinking did!' he laughed.

I laughed back. He seems much more jovial now he's got his freedom back. I hope he stays that way. When things quietened down a bit I decided to make my call.

'Good afternoon. Could I speak to someone regarding an incident at Brookwood station on the night of 13/14th July please?'

'Wait a moment.'

The female voice came over as quite rude and abrupt. Just then another lady came on to the phone.

'Can I help you?'

'I was wondering if someone could help me regarding an incident at Brookwood station on the night of 13/14th July please.'

'Oh yes, we had a lot of calls about that but it's all gone quiet now. What do you need to know?'

'I'm just calling for an update to enable me to complete my story.'

'Well what I have here says that it might be a hoax and the BTP have closed the case. We did have a separate report that a ghost was seen on the platform but of course as you can appreciate, we've dismissed that as complete nonsense and all had a great laugh.'

'What's happening with the driver?'

'That matter is being dealt with internally and I'm afraid I can't give you any more information on that.'

I then wondered if I should tell her about the latest information that I had just received. Perhaps I should.

'I've just been speaking to Sergeant Banger of the BTP and he has confirmed that they are now investigating a report or at least a theory that the incident was actually a stunt pulled off by persons unknown in order to recreate a suicide which had occurred at the station on the corresponding date in 1931. I suggest that someone from your company should talk to the police. I've previously spoken with the driver and I'm fully aware of the effect all this has had on him.'

'That does throw a whole new light on things. I'll have to speak to our Operations Director and of course the BTP to get all this confirmed. So what are you planning to put in your story?'

'I'm not sure yet. It's been quite awhile now since the initial incident. I'll have to run all this latest information past my editor again but she's keen for me to get the story finished by the end of this week.'

'Good luck with that!'

'Sorry, to whom have I been speaking with please?'

'I'm Suzanne Mountjoy; I'm the press officer for the South West Division,'

'Okay, thank you. It's been a pleasure speaking with you.'

She was quite pleasant and easy to talk to. I'm glad I was able to give her an update and I hope she passes that on to the appropriate people. I think this new take on things will certainly help the driver, that's if he gets to hear about it. Perhaps I should contact him myself. Now to get on with writing the story but I think I need to speak to Nancy again first. KNOCK, KNOCK!

'Come!'

'Hello, I've just spoken to the police and the railway. The police have confirmed that they are now treating the incident as a stunt as Phil Janner has suggested and the railway are also now aware.' I said.

'Well that puts a whole new slant on things. I suggest you move your feature forward with the hoax angle, ensure that you engage the readers; get them to write in with their own views or something. You could do that in your 'sign off' paragraph. That way it will give you the possibility of writing up another item on the same story if and when anything progresses. Is that Okay?'

'Yes, Nancy, thank you!'

'Now piss off out of my office and get the fucking story finished!'

'Err, yes Nancy, thank you I will.'

When I got back to my desk I reached for my mug, coffee? Then I thought no. I looked at the clock. I thought I might go for a drink somewhere and then come back here about 7pm but then what if Nancy and Mr Hackett are at it again? Maybe it's best if I try and come in first thing in the morning. The first train from Farnham to Woking leaves at 5:12am. Perhaps I should rough out my story when I get home this evening and then come in and type it up early tomorrow. Good Idea I thought!

Back home I cracked open a bottle of *Vin de Pays du Gard*, stuck on some Pink Floyd and sat down in the corner. Time to get writing and put this thing together but where do I start?

I've had to change it around enough already. I need to make sure I keep it concise and that I remember to ask those open questions. Everything is still a bit of a mish-mash at the moment.

19

I fell asleep before I wrote anything last night, now I feel the pressure mounting and I'm beginning to question my own ability as a newspaper reporter and ask myself if I'm actually in the right job? I can feel the depression slowly coming back. I haven't felt this down for a few weeks and I don't really want to go to work this morning. I just want to hide myself away somewhere. I'm so tempted to phone in sick but a little voice in my head is preventing me, the voice of sensibility and rationalism, and the reassuring voice which keeps me sane in my moments of darkness is telling me to snap out of it. I eventually decide to get up, combat the mirror and get myself ready for work.

The train only has four carriages this morning so I have to stand all the way to Woking and it's all a bit of a squeeze. I recognise the guard, it's Bill Ashcroft. Again we acknowledge each other but he has trouble walking through because of all the standing passengers. When I got off the train at Woking he called me over.

'Hey Jack, Steve Callion's back at work today, he got the all important call yesterday. He's on light duties at the office in Woking and expects to be back out on the track soon. The Drivers' Inspector is taking him out on the mainline next week as he needs to be passed out again,' he said.

'Passed out?'

'Yes, tested as competent on that line of route, its normal practice after someone's been involved in an incident.'

'Well that's great news, please send him my regards,' I said.

I helped put a spring in my step and wondered if my call to the railway had had any influence at all. I remember Phil Janner's theory that is was all an elaborate hoax, perhaps this is what's helped Steve to get his job back. Maybe his managers have started to believe him now. This news has cheered me up a bit but I still have to write my story up and I'm still not sure how.

In the office Beryl and Geoff were talking about Alfie, the new freelance.

'Where's he from?' asked Geoff.

'Mauritius I believe.' Beryl answered.

'Where's that?'

'On the other side of Africa, at least 6,000 miles away I'd say. His mum is actually English. He told me that his parents met when she was out there on holiday in the 60s.'

'I don't even know his surname,' I said.

'It's Nubeebuckus,' said Beryl.

'It's an odd name but quite common out there I believe.'

Geoff shrugged his shoulders, 'Yeah, that's all well and good but he's only been here five minutes and he's already nicking all the best stories.'

We all laughed.

'Time to make the coffee I think,' shrieked Beryl.

As she went off to the kitchen I went back to my desk. I needed to find the time to work on my story and was hoping the office would be quiet today. Geoff just said he was off out to cover a story about a woman with a rare cancer condition in St John's and no-one else was expected in today apart from Nancy much later.

'You'll have Beryl to keep you company, watch her though, she's a bit of a dark horse that one!' said Geoff.

'I heard that!' retorted Beryl.

We all laughed again. When Geoff left I decided to tell Beryl about my anxiety over writing the story and that I was worried that I may not be able to get it done in time.

'Don't worry, look, the office is very quiet today. Nancy's at an editorial seminar in Southampton and won't be back for a few hours yet. I'm going to sneak over to Guildford and do some shopping and if I see you with your head down working when I get back I'll promise to leave you alone.'

Just then Ted and Alfie walked in. That's the end of that idea I thought.

'We're off to court, I'm showing Alfie the ropes; we'll be back here in the morning.'

That's a relief. I was worried that they'd be in the office all day. I would have had no chance of getting anything done. I'm still trying to work out how to write my story up but at least I should have some peace and quiet soon but now the phone rings.

'Is that Jack?'
'Yes, who's that?'
'Carol from the *Farnham Herald*.'
'Oh, hello Carol, sorry I didn't recognise your voice.'
'Don't worry; I've got a few sniffles this week. I just wanted to let you know that Steve Callion the train driver is back at work and I was wondering how you got on with your story. It's just that I haven't seen anything yet.'
'That's strange, I'm sat here now and just about to start writing it all. I saw Bill Ashcroft earlier, he was the guard on my train to work this morning and he told me that Steve is back at work.'
'Yes it is good news. Do you still need any help with your article?'
'To be honest the big problem I've had is all the distractions. Without saying too much I now have an angle to work on, I just need to know where to start and then everything should be Okay.'
'That's good; just remember that I'm only a phone call away should you need anything.'
'I will, and thanks again.'
When I put the phone down I remembered what Nancy had said about working too closely with reporters from other newspapers. I was careful not to let on about the hoax angle. I also have the impression that Carol may have run her story in the *Farnham Herald* already which is why she sounded quite a bit surprised when I said I was still writing mine. I decided to dig out a copy of the *Tribune* which reported the initial incident. It doesn't say a lot, I remember mentioning a suspected suicide and reporting the knock on delays and cancellations. It came on deadline day so was a bit hurried. All the other stuff started to emerge later.

After two or three very peaceful hours I think I now have my story ready at last. It's quite long, about 650 words but that should fit a double page spread if a photograph is included. It may be too optimistic to think that Nancy will put anything on the front page now but a little header somewhere would be good. I want to show my story to Amanda; I think she will be very proud of me. She'll be glad though that everything was just a hoax. Now the phone rings again.

'Can I speak to Jack Compton please?'

'Speaking, this is Jack.'

'Hello, I'm Detective Constable Harry Naughton from the Surrey Constabulary. I'm investigating an incident which occurred on the night of 13/14th July and was wondering if you can assist me with my enquiries.'

'I'll try.'

'The case has been passed on to me my British Transport colleagues. I understand that you've been speaking to someone called Phil who told you that the incident was fabricated as part of some kind of hoax.'

'Yes, you're talking about Phil Janner; he's a local historian and is quite high up on the residents' association in Knaphill. He has a theory and that's where the story about the hoax has come from.'

'Well we have our own theory but what is complicating the issue is the chap who works on the platform.'

'Which chap?'

'Wilbur White, the porter.'

'Why?'

'There was an alleged incident on the station three days ago where a man spoke to a woman and then simply disappeared. She thought he had fallen on to the track but nothing was found. It was captured on the CCTV but unfortunately the image isn't very clear. Mr White told us it was the same man that you had been asking him about.'

'Reginald Smythe?'

'Yes, that's the name he gave us. Do you know anything more about him?'

'I wish I did. The reason I've been asking questions is because I believe he's actually a ghost. I know it all sounds a bit strange but the only record I could find of him dates back to October 1929 and then the following month he's found dead in a well. He was a patient at the old asylum.'

'Brookwood?'

'Yes.'

'How do you know all this?'

'He's mentioned in one of my grandfather's old diaries. He was a patient there at the same time. My grandfather later joined the RAF and was a hero in the Second World War,' I said rather proudly.

'Fascinating but can you give me any clearer details about this Smythe chap?'

'No, not really. I've spent a long time trying already and I kept drawing blanks. I think you really need to speak to Phil Janner, he seems to have access to lots of local records both past and present.'

'Don't worry, I will.'

'Would you like his number?'

'Ah, no it's alright, I've managed to find it whilst we've been talking, his details are jumping out at me for some reason and I don't know why but that's strictly a police matter. Thank you for your time anyway. Good day to you.'

After I put the phone down I felt that the police officer was a bit abrupt and didn't really want to listen to what I was saying. Just then the front office door opened and Nancy came in.

'Jack what are you still doing here, shouldn't you be on your way home by now?'

'I was, I had just finished my story on the Brookwood incident and then the phone rang.'

'Let me see it then!'

She grabbed the two A4 pages out of hand and sat down in Geoff's chair and lit a cigarette.

'Don't worry, it's after office hours, it doesn't matter now,' she said.

She appeared to read my article two or three times.

'Pass me a pen, quickly.'

She then crossed out most of my first paragraph and then scribbled all down one side.

'The substance of what you're trying to say is all here but some of it is simply back to front. You need to draw readers to the story straight away. You must make sure that the important stuff is always at the beginning. Leave the suppositions, questions and contact requests to the end. In fact you don't need to include any contact requests, they're irrelevant. Just stick to the facts!'

'Thank you,' I said rather anxiously.

'I'm an editor, that's my job; it's just that if you get it right in the first place it makes my job a lot easier. Just retype it in the morning and make sure it's on my desk by ten o'clock. Now fuck off, I've got things to do.'

As I was leaving the office I saw Mr Hackett struggling to park his car in the bay outside. No wonder she was in a hurry to get rid of me I thought.

20

Finally I've been able to get my feature story finished, it seems so long ago since the incident originally occurred and now it's finally sitting in the tray on Nancy's desk waiting to be published. At least she's seen it and I've made the changes that she suggested. Hopefully I can relax at last even though I still have many unanswered questions of my own about the incident. I need to find out more. I need to know if the spirit of Maisie really does exist and what about the ghost of Reginald Smythe? I definitely need to find out more about him!

New Hoax Theory behind Brookwood Station Incident

Following the incident at Brookwood Railway Station where a train was involved in a so-called phantom fatality our reporter Jack Compton has been investigating...

Late into the evening of Wednesday 13th July a train driver reported hitting and killing someone as he was passing through Brookwood Station but a body was never found. The train had been taken out of service at Woking and was being moved to the engine shed at Farnham for repairs when the incident happened at around 8:45pm.

Police and other emergency services were called to the scene and searched the area which caused major disruption for passengers for the rest of the evening and late into the following day. Many trains had to be cancelled while others were diverted via Guildford.

British Transport Police originally closed their file on the incident after the train driver who cannot be named for legal reasons was removed from his post on medical grounds. Police however are now investigating a theory that the incident was an elaborate hoax set up by a secret sect made up of staff who once worked at Brookwood Hospital.

On 13th July 1931 a young female patient escaped from what was then known as The Brookwood Asylum and ran on to the tracks at Brookwood Station. She was reportedly killed outright by a train which was taking passengers from Waterloo to the docks at Southampton. The incident occurred at 8:45pm!

Brookwood Hospital in Knaphill is currently in the process of closing as a result of the well publicised Care in the Community reforms but administration staff at the hospital told the *Tribune* that some files and patient records from 1931 are missing.

Wendy Rance, Chief Clerk at the hospital said, "There was a group of auxiliary staff who worked here until about ten years ago. They formed a secret sect called the Shadow-Masters; it was a bit like a Free Mason's society. They used to meet in the crypt under the chapel until they were found out. Gradually they all dispersed and the group disbanded. No-one really knew who was in the group; it was all a bit weird."

Detectives from the Surrey Constabulary have now taken over enquiries from their British Transport Police colleagues but are keeping an open mind while investigations continue.

The incident has drawn much public attention and paranormal experts have been in a frenzy ever since. The ghost of a man believed to be connected with the original incident has been reported at the station but his sighting has now been dismissed as part of the hoax but many questions still remain unanswered.

One expert is the well known Isle of Wight based psychic medium and former TV personality Esther Whitehawk who firmly believes that the incident in July was a recurring paranormal event and that the train driver was simply susceptible to the presence of spirit.

She exclusively told the *Tribune*, "Spirits are those trapped between this world and the next and who make their presence felt through noises or smells. Of course there are the occasional sightings as well. They may be people with unfinished business here. People have told me that they've heard footsteps in the station, or noticed the smell of tobacco when no-one else is around. I do always look for a rational explanation first. If someone feels a cold breeze, for example, it could be just a draught. I understand that many people are dismissive of stories of ghosts and spirits but I do accept that some people are more receptive than others."

Other experts have also been to visit the scene including the Reverend Nathanial Bream from the *Fortean Times* who has in part agreed with Ms Whitehawk's comments. He is continuing with his own investigation and believes there is a more rational explanation although he is dismissive of the hoax theory.

Suzanne Mountjoy, press officer at Network Southeast stated, "We have had a lot of calls about the incident but everything has all gone quiet now."

She was unaware the whole incident may have simply been a hoax and said that she would pass that information on to the appropriate department at British Rail for internal investigation.

* We would be interested to know what our readers think about the ghostly goings-on at Brookwood Station. Please write to us at the *Woking Tribune*, PO Box 149, Woking, Surrey, GU21 6EJ.

'Jack, Jack!' It was Nancy calling, 'Into my office NOW!' she shouted excitedly.

I was a bit taken aback and now I was worried what she was going to say about my article. When I entered the office she was waving it above her head.

'Sit down, sit down. Look here, what you've written is fine and what we have here now could be ongoing, mark my word, there will be more coming out on this, especially if the police find out who might be behind the hoax.'

'I'm still not sure if it was a hoax, I'm keeping an open mind on that.' I said.

'Well keep an open mind but don't waste any more time on the story unless you have something concrete. If something else comes up then good but let's just let it rest for now.'

'So will it make the front page this week?' I asked.

'No, unfortunately not.'

'Why?'

'Alfie's story will be on Page One, he's got the scoop.'

'Scoop?'

'Yes, the attempted murder story. The victim died last night so it's actually a murder investigation now. The woman was stabbed three times in the back by her step-son. It's already been on the radio this morning so it really is hot news.'

'Well that's bad timing, there hasn't been a murder in Woking for ages.'

'Perhaps if you hadn't have dragged your heels so much then maybe we could have put your story on to the front page a couple of weeks ago instead of all that usual political rubbish we keep getting from the local councillors. You really do need to speed up with your writing. You still need to interrogate your copy and ensure that it's accurate and that may help you file your stories in time for the deadlines. Now fuck off out of my sight. Oh, and by the way, on the whole this is a very good little feature, so well done.'

When I came out of Nancy's office my ears felt red raw. Everyone was looking at me so I decided to just walk past them all and come out for a stroll. I found my usual bench on the canal towpath. The sun was trying to shine and there was laughter and singing coming from the crew of a passing narrowboat. Time to relax at last I thought.

21

Friday 2nd September and the paper with my feature article is finally out, quite a few weeks since the incident. Alfie's story is on the front page with a picture of the victim. I eventually find my article on page seven. Two more of my smaller articles are further inside. It's the first time I've had three of my stories in one issue but Geoff and Ted are always filling the news pages up with all their stuff. Apart from the four sports pages at the back everything is really just advertising. I remember Beryl telling me that its people like Jasmine in the advertising office who really keep the paper ticking over and drawing in the revenue.

'Without them, there would be no paper,' I remember her telling me.

Time now to look for a new story but I've decided to spend this weekend trying to uncover a bit more of my family tree. Tomorrow I'm meeting Jayne for a drink, on Saturday I plan to visit Amanda and on Sunday I'm going to walk from Farnham to Tilford and try and find Maisie's grave at the All Saints Church. I just hope the weather stays fine for me now.

22

I met with Jayne at The Sovereigns. It was quite a mild evening so we sat outside. She was telling me about her love for red wine and how her mother probably weaned her on to it when she was still a child.

'Mum probably got a thrill out of trying to make me sick,' she laughed.

We spoke about all the inevitable things which connected us. It was obvious that neither of us knew too much about our father. Everything seemed to skip a generation back and she was intrigued when I told her all that I had found out about Tommy.

'He's definitely the grandfather I never knew I had,' she said.

I suggested that she should visit Amanda one day but Jayne was too busy with other plans which had been arranged for quite awhile.

'I'm visiting her tomorrow; perhaps I can arrange something then.'

'Does she know about me?'

'Of course she does, I think it's where all the secrecy about our family stems from. Getting two women pregnant at the same time was very taboo in the 60s, it still is and I know it brought great shame on the family. Sometimes Amanda can sound even more posh than the Queen even with her gravelly voice. I think she had certain values around that time although they've almost certainly disappeared as she's got older.'

'She's mellowed then!'

'That's one way of putting it. She's only in her 60s though, but she looks so much older. She drinks lots of brandy and smokes like a trooper. She still comes over a little nervous and can be quite abrupt sometimes, especially if it's something to do with the family. She's still very guarded about it.'

'Well yes, I would love to meet her at some point. After all, she is a member of my family as well.'

'Yes she most certainly is,' I chortled.

'Do you always drink this much?'

'Only when I'm nervous.'

'So it runs in the family then! You needn't be nervous of me, I'm your sister don't forget.'

'Yes, I know and that is something I'm still trying to get used to. I'm so glad I found you.'

'I'm glad you found me too.'

Jayne had arranged for her husband Dave to pick her up at 8.30pm. He's been swimming with the kids. I decided to stay behind for just one more drink on my own before getting my train back to Farnham. It was starting to get chilly and the pub had filled up by then. It all was very boisterous as people started to enjoy their weekend.

23

I got to Amanda's house just before noon. She was already cooking dinner, sausages, eggs and fried sliced potatoes.

'It's always a fry-up on Saturdays. Sit down, I've laid the table,' she said.

I always sit in the same place, in my usual chair and there is always an air of nostalgia when I come back. Memories of childhood all seem to return when I sit in this room. It's probably because nothing has changed much. Just a new television set in the corner and a CD player on the side. I don't think my poor auntie has even got any music to play on it yet.

I told her about my meeting with Jayne last night and how well we seem to be getting on. I suggested that I might bring her over for a visit soon. I told her about what happened to her first husband Mark, and about Dave and their children. She seemed quite absorbed in everything I was telling her.'

'Yes it's about time I met the young lady. None of what happened was ever her fault. It wasn't yours either. I'm not too sure about having her little brats running about my house though.'

I laughed.

'Don't worry, I'm only joking,' she said as she broke into a smile.

I told her that I was planning on walking from Farnham to Tilford tomorrow. It's a nice walk but some of the roads near Tilford can be quite dangerous as there's no pavement.

'Why are you going to Tilford?'

'To visit Maisie's grave.'

'Maisie?'

'Yes Maisie, the lady who Tommy mentions in his diaries, you told me that he went there when he came back for my father's funeral in 1966.'

'Sorry, I keep forgetting her name. Yes he did but why would you want to go there?'

'To pay my respects, he obviously loved her and I still have some unanswered questions about something else.'

'Something else?'

'Something to do with this story I've been working on.'
I had taken a cutting of my story from this week's paper and gave it to Amanda. We both went very quiet as she read the article. I wondered how she might respond.

'Jack, are you telling me that you think Maisie has returned from the dead and jumped in front of that poor man's train.'

'That's exactly what I think. Something very strange happened. I purposely left my own views out of the article and stuck to the facts. That was on my editor's advice. I still think that there is something more to this and I need to find the answer.'

'I'm not sure how Tommy would feel if he knew you were meddling in this, I think he would turn in his grave.'

'To be honest I think he does know. I think Maisie is trying to connect with him through me. The psychic medium who has been involved with the story told me once that Maisie's spirit was standing next to me'

'Stop it; you're making me go cold.'

'Sorry, I just want to be honest with you and tell you everything.'

'When Mr Meredith brought over that tin full of Tommy's things I was shocked. Yes, of course I read everything but never really understood why he was in that awful place. It seems he didn't either. What happened between him and that Maisie was very sad but he went on to marry Katherine and they had a very happy life. Your bloody father was the result!'

'I just think visiting Maisie's grave may be the last piece in my jigsaw. I feel like I'm being drawn to it and I can almost feel her spirit inside me now. I think Esther Whitehawk has had an indirect influence on me. It's just something I need to do even if I don't find the answers I'm look for.'

'But what is it you're looking for, what answers?'

'To find out if there really is life after death I suppose. To find out if the spirit of Maisie really does exist. To find out if it really was her who ran across in front of that train. I just need to find out if there is any truth in what Esther Whitehawk has been telling me,' I said.

'Well good luck. I'm trying not to be sceptical but after getting Tommy's diaries and letters back after all those years, nothing really surprises me anymore.'

24

This morning when I opened curtains the sun was shining. It was just what I had been hoping for, a bright sunny day for my walk over to Tilford. I stopped off at the café in East Street for a bacon roll and a coffee. I had thought about a full English breakfast but the place was full of Irish builders and their cigarette smoke, it wasn't too comfortable so I just ate my roll quickly, poured my coffee from a mug into a polystyrene cup and left. The weather was actually quite warm; it felt as if the summer was having one last encore before the autumn comes. I felt a bit tired but began to wake up the more I got into my stride.

The walk took just over two hours. Fortunately the roads weren't too busy, just a few vintage buses going by which was quite interesting. When I reached the village green I walked over to the river and sat on a bench near the bridge. I could see quite a few trout struggling against the flow of the water. It reminded me of something Amanda said when I was growing up, 'Never go with the flow, only dead fish go with the flow!' Her words were always quite profound. I decided to walk over to the Barley Mow, the pub that Phil Janner had mentioned. Someone was playing bar-billiards and a radio was on. An old man was serving behind the bar and kept looking at me a bit funny.

'I haven't seen you in here before lad, are you old enough for this?'

'Yes, of course, I'm twenty-eight; well just anyway, I had my birthday in July.'

'Twenty-eight? You don't look a day over twenty-seven.'

It was then that I realised he was joking with me and that made me feel quite relaxed. I took my pint and sat at the table outside. Once I had remembered where the church was I finished my pint and then made my way across the green.

Walking into the churchyard everything seemed to go quiet rather quickly. There was a blackbird singing and some squirrels scuffling between some tombstones searching for nuts. When I walked around to the back of the church I saw there were some slightly newer graves, one was of an old priest who had once been the vicar at the church, Parson Jaggs who had died in 1973, his name seemed familiar but I couldn't remember where I had seen it before. The older graves were covered in lichen and moss. I could hear someone cutting away at something in the background; it was a CLIP, CLIP, CLIP sound. I then saw a very old lady with reddish greying hair stand up between two of the headstones and she began walking over towards me. She seemed to be quite curious probably because I was holding a camera.

'Good afternoon young man, can I help you?'

'Yes, perhaps you can, I'm looking for a grave, a grave of someone who died in 1931.'

'All the graves from around that time are over to the west of the churchyard,' she said pointing.

I walked over and sensed that she was following me. Most of the graves in the section were unmarked. For some reason I was drawn to one grave in particular. I knelt down and wondered who was buried beneath and then decided to look at all the graves with headstones to see if I could find Maisie. I couldn't find anything so I thought that she must be in one of the unmarked plots. The old lady sidled up beside me.

'Any luck?' she asked.

'No, not yet, I don't think the person I'm looking for has a headstone.' I said.

'If you go into the church there's a cabinet to the side of the vestry, in there you will find some old scrolls and some books. There is also a map of the graveyard. It tells you who's buried in each of the plots from 1867 right up until 1973. Parson Jaggs was the last person to update the map, but there haven't been many burials since he passed over to the other side anyway,' she said.

I went into the church. Sunlight was shining through the stained-glass window on to the altar. There were vases of fresh flowers everywhere, all with bright colours but I felt an unnerving calm about the place. It felt like ghosts were watching me from every corner, from every pew inside the church. The old lady followed me in.

'I can't let you remove the map, there are no copies; you must look at it here. We can't afford to lose it,' she said rather anxiously.
Not once had she asked me who I was looking for.
'Have you thought of having a copy made?' I asked.
'Many times, but the current vicar here is a procrastinator and he doesn't behold modern technology whatever that's supposed to mean. I think he's waiting for someone to volunteer and draw up another handmade copy,' she said.
Eventually I opened up the map. It showed the pathways between the graves and the most predominant trees. The graves were shown as rectangles, each had a name, or two if a man and wife had been buried together.
'Six feet under for one and another three feet on top for the double graves,' the old lady remarked.
The date of burial was written next to a reference number.
'The reference number refers to the parish register, that would hold the person's date of birth and date of death,' she said.
Just as she was saying that I found Maisie's name. It showed the date of burial as 21st July 1931, that's about a week after she died at Brookwood. I made a note of where the grave was, folded the map, placed it back on the shelf and went back outside. When I got to the grave I realised that it was the same one I had knelt beside earlier. The old lady was standing behind me.
'This is the grave that I saw you kneeling beside before. Isn't it?'
'Yes, I was drawn to it straight away for some reason.'
'Do you know the person?'
'Obviously not, she died in 1931 and I wasn't born until 1966!'
'Sorry, let me rephrase that, do you know of this person or are you related to her.'
'I know of her, she was a friend of my grandfather's.'
'Yes, I know, a very dear friend.'
'How do you know?'
'I just do. Your grandfather was Thomas Compton; everyone just called him Tommy.'
'Yes but how do you know all this, did you know Maisie?'
'Maisie Albright? Of course I know Maisie.'

Just then there was a gust of wind. It was quite random as the whole day had been very still with hardly any breeze at all. When I turned to speak to the old lady again she was gone.

Then I heard the CLIP, CLIP, CLIP sound again, this time it was coming from the other side of the churchyard but it faded as I walked over. There was no sign of her. I walked back into the church but again, she was nowhere to be seen. It was all a bit odd and I didn't really want to leave without thanking her for her for all her help. I also wanted to ask her how she knew Maisie and Tommy; perhaps she was at the asylum at the same time. She'd be about the same age they would have been now if they were both still alive.

Eventually I left and decided to go back to the pub. The same man was still serving behind the bar and another old man who was wearing dark rimmed glasses with amber coloured lenses and a black beret was sat by the door with his dog.

'Back again?' said the barman.

'Yes, I need another drink.'

'You alright lad?'

'Yes, I think so. I've just come back from the church. I've been looking for an old grave.'

'Did you find it?'

'Yes, I did, thanks to an old lady who was tending to the other graves over there.'

'Oh, that would be Miss Albright. You only ever see her scurrying about over there, never anywhere else,' said the man by the door.

'Miss Albright?'

'Yes,' said the barman. 'The old girl Maisie, she's a bit of an odd one but like my old mate just said, you only ever see her over there, never anywhere else, she's been there for as long as I can remember, I don't even know where she lives.'

I had to put my drink down and walked out of the pub rather quickly. I moved on to the village green. I thought about going back to the church but something was holding me back. A strange wind was picking up and it was almost as if I could hear voices, I did hear a voice, a young woman's voice!

'Thank you, thank you; thank you!'

And then the wind just stopped as quickly as it came.

The sound of the traffic became more dominant and it felt as if I had been transported back to reality from somewhere else. I couldn't explain it; it was all over in seconds.

When I got home I decided to phone Esther Whitehawk and tell her what had happened today.

'Hello, this is Jack.'

'Jack?'

'Yes, Jack, Jack Compton from the *Woking Tribune.*'

'Oh, Hello Jack.'

I told her everything that I had experienced from the moment I stepped into the churchyard and hoped that she would be able to offer an explanation.

'I think Maisie has been trying to make contact with Tommy, she's possibly been using you as some kind of vessel so that she can somehow be with him again. Perhaps she's now finally succeeded!'

'But what about the old lady at the church, I went into the nearby pub and people there knew who she was, they even knew her name was Maisie?'

'Even I can't explain that one. I would give Nathaniel Bream a ring, he would know more about that sort of thing than I do but don't trust everything he says.'

I thanked Esther for her time and then phoned Nathaniel and told him everything that had happened.

'It sounds like your imagination has been running wild but there will always be a rational explanation and sometimes we need to fly back and purify as it were and cleanse our senses. There's a lot of research going on and much of this can be just a state of mind, particularly if someone has been experiencing psychological issues. I'm secretly working on a feature at the moment where neuroscientists have succeeded in creating ghosts in a laboratory by tricking the brains of test subjects into feeling an unexpected presence in the room. The experiment is designed to conjure up a ghostly illusion and has proved once and for all that it's only our mind playing tricks. The semi-visible or invisible, creepy presence reported by so many people over the centuries is just a set of mixed-up signals in the brain and that's what probably happened to the train driver at Brookwood,' he confided.

'Do you think the same thing has been happening to me?'

'Yes almost certainly.'

'But what about the old lady in the graveyard at Tilford; other people have seen her, was she a ghost?'

'No, like I just said. There aren't any ghosts; it's all in the mind.'

I thanked Nathaniel for his time but wasn't convinced by his explanation or perhaps I just didn't want to believe him. Even Esther wasn't much help this time so now I am left to wonder!

After a while I poured myself a glass of wine and walked outside, the sky was clear and the moon was low. The stars seemed brighter than usual and a magpie was sitting on the back fence. I had never seen a magpie at this time of the night before and I gave it a quick salute before it flew off and up into a tree. Saluting magpies has always been a family thing. Something Tommy I think had mentioned in one of his diaries.

Printed in Great Britain
by Amazon